# Right Cowboy, Right Time

 Horseshoe Home Ranch

# LIZ ISAACSON

ISBN-13: 978-1-63876-242-3

"Fear not: for they that be with us are more than they that be with them."

— 2 KINGS 6:16

# CHAPTER 1

"Oh, chips!" Caleb Chamberlain swung the overflowing shopping cart around, several boxes of frozen waffles falling off the top. Ty scooped one up and lifted it back over his shoulder like a football.

"Go long!"

Caleb didn't hesitate. His cowboy boots slipped a little on the tile in the grocery store and his injured leg gave him a bit of trouble, but he got his feet under him soon enough. He sprinted down the frozen foods aisle, glancing over his shoulder when he heard Ty grunt.

He put on a burst of speed to be able to get under the waffle box, reaching...reaching until he pulled it in and tucked it under his arm. A laugh spilled from his mouth as he slid to a stop, the old injury in his lower leg and ankle throbbing just a little. The moms with kids stared at him, and one elderly lady Caleb recognized from church frowned.

He tipped his cowboy hat as they went back to selecting milk and eggs and yogurt, then trotted back to where Ty was still picking fallen waffle boxes from the ground. "That was awesome." Caleb balanced the waffle-football on top of their haul. "But we forgot the chips and Gloria is makin' taco soup tomorrow night."

Getting grocery duty in February was every cowhand's dream, so Caleb wasn't overly concerned about hurrying to get the corn chips. He'd probably even suggest he and Ty stop by the deli to get a soft serve cone before they headed back up the canyon to Horseshoe Home Ranch.

No sense in getting back in time to get another assignment. Not in such chilly weather. Even the grocery store had their usually open front area closed today, because the wind howled like it had a personal vendetta against the Montana town of Gold Valley.

Sometimes it felt that way to Caleb, and he wondered why he still lived here. But he couldn't think of anywhere else he'd rather be. His parents lived here; his younger sister cut hair at the salon; his twin brother had only one more year in Michigan to finish his dentistry degree, then he'd return to open a practice.

Caleb had worked at Horseshoe Home since he was fourteen years old, with only a brief hiatus after he recovered from his car accident, and he didn't see anything changing for the next dozen years.

"Pretty girls up ahead," Ty hissed out of the corner of his mouth, causing Caleb to stop using the shopping cart like it was a scooter.

The three girls walking toward them could hardly have graduated from high school. In fact, in Caleb's best estimation, they were probably still *in* high school. Ty, though the same age as Caleb, looked and acted like a teenager, and could probably get away with dating an eighteen-year-old. But Caleb, who looked all of his twenty-six years, could not.

Didn't even want to.

He wasn't really looking for a new girlfriend, not since the disaster that had been Robin Melcher. Oh, no. Caleb was still trying to rebuild what she'd knocked down five years ago, and it wasn't going that well. Definitely better than when he used to drown himself in alcohol, and exponentially better than healing from an accident stemming from his drinking. So his recovery was probably going better than he thought.

Still, he averted his eyes when Ty said, "Afternoon, ladies," and kept on toward the snack food aisle. Ty was exceptionally good at making women feel special, like he'd known them their whole lives. He'd been one of Caleb's best friends growing up, their friendship cemented for life after Caleb had driven himself off the road and into a cement barrier.

Caleb and Ty had actually known most of the available women in Gold Valley his whole life. None of them were interested in him, and Robin's poisoned words flashed through his mind.

*You're going nowhere, Caleb Chamberlain.*

She had a sweet, sticky, soprano voice that twanged on

his name, even as he pushed her and her parting words to him from his mind.

He was going nowhere, but that wasn't the problem. The real problem was that going nowhere was just fine with him. He didn't want to leave Gold Valley and Horseshoe Home Ranch, even if he dreamed of being a cowboy in warmer Texas or Oklahoma.

He didn't care if no one was interested. He felt content with his life at the moment, and though he needed to get his self-confidence back where it used to be, he knew a woman wouldn't help with that.

"Nathan!"

He glanced up at the mention of his twin's name. He was used to being mistaken for his twin, as they shared the exact same DNA. Same sandy brown hair. Same dark brown eyes. They even walked with an identical gait.

The similarities ended there. Nathan was driven, and successful, and married now with a baby. Caleb had graduated in agricultural sciences while working at the ranch, where...he still worked. He did just fine, in his opinion, but when compared with Nathan, Caleb definitely paled.

Before he could actually locate the source of who'd called Nathan's name, a woman launched herself into his arms.

"Oof," he grunted as he stumbled backward. Without thinking, he put his hands around the woman, mostly to keep himself from falling down. She smelled like flowers and soap, and Caleb's heart pounced into his throat.

She stepped back in a flurry of black hair, which she

smoothed back to reveal even darker eyes and olive colored skin. She wore a lot of black makeup around her eyes, and Caleb thought she looked exotic. He swallowed and found his throat exceptionally dry.

Beautiful and exotic, a dangerous combination to Caleb's bachelor life.

"It's Holly," she said. "Holly Gray?"

The name struck a bell in Caleb's head, but he couldn't place her. "I was Katherine's best friend in high school?"

Katherine—his younger sister.

Ty nudged him, and Caleb's voice thawed enough for him to emit a strangled chuckle. "Oh, right. Katie."

Her eyes searched his. "I didn't know you were back in town."

"Well, I'm not—" Caleb started, his voice muting when Ty thumped him on the back.

"He's back," Ty said.

Caleb usually enjoyed this game of pretend-to-be-some-one-you're-not, but this time he cast Ty a glare. He turned back to Holly, distracted by her curvy hips and slim waist. "I guess I never really left."

She smiled, a short laugh escaping her dark red lips. Caleb couldn't look away, and he realized he hadn't been in a relationship for too long. His brain searched for how long, but it was being slow and dumb.

"It feels that way, doesn't it?" Holly glanced back to where she'd left her cart. "This town does have some sort of magic, though, doesn't it?" She looked at him, and he realized she'd asked two questions.

"Yeah." He answered them both at the same time and immediately cursed himself for sounding like he'd forgotten how to breathe.

"So what brings you back to town?" Ty asked, stepping slightly in front of Caleb.

Caleb had no idea if Holly had actually left town. His life now pretty much existed up the canyon, on the ranch. It always had, but when Robin had left him, he'd made the thirty-minute drive as often as he necessary to procure the liquor he needed to erase her from his mind.

Now, with that behind him, and his leg fully healed, he came down for church if the roads were good and he didn't have chores to do. And, of course, if he pulled grocery duty.

Holly tossed her curls over her shoulder. "Oh, you know. This and that."

Caleb cocked an eyebrow at her. "How long have you been gone?"

"Five years."

*Five years, five years.* Caleb tried to think of why Holly Gray would've been mixed up with Nathan five years ago. Recalling his brother's life when his own had been so tumultuous was harder than Caleb liked. He'd been really removed from everyone and everything while dating Robin.

It hit him at the same time Holly leaned forward and kissed his cheek. "We should catch up sometime." She gave him a coy smile, turned, and sashayed back to her cart. She didn't turn and look back, something Caleb was grateful for.

He didn't want her to see how he'd gone still, his mouth hanging open. Ty elbowed him and said, "Who was *that?*"

Caleb swallowed as feeling returned to his muscles. "That was Holly Gray," he said in a monotone. "My twin brother's ex-fiancé."

———

By the time Caleb got back to the ranch, unloaded all the food, and helped Ty divvy it all up, his patience had reached it's end. He needed to call Nathan *now*.

Ty had made some suggestions about Holly, none of which Caleb particularly wanted to entertain—except maybe the part where he'd said Caleb should *definitely* call her and *definitely* get caught up with her.

But Caleb needed to talk to Nathan first. He'd left his groceries at the administration lodge, his breath practically freezing in the air before him, and had taken three steps toward his cabin when Jace called his name.

Caleb groaned inwardly, but turned back to the foreman. "Yeah, boss?"

"Any trouble in town?" Jace leaned against the pillar like he didn't feel the negative temperatures. Maybe he didn't.

"No," Caleb said, his voice automatically going up in pitch. "No trouble." He was so used to denying any wrongdoing, and he'd gotten really good at talking his way out of a mess.

"I shouldn't have sent you and Ty together." Jace sighed.

"I knew that." He finally pinned his gaze on Caleb. "Throwing frozen waffles down the aisle? Really?"

"I didn't throw any waffles." Caleb held up his hands. "I swear." A grin tugged at the corners of his mouth, and he worked to flatten them before the all-seeing eye of Jace Lovell could see.

"What about the rumor of two cowboys wrestling in front of the pretzels?" Jace cocked his head to the side.

"That was nothing," Caleb said. "Ty said my ears were stickin' out, and I elbowed him, and he maybe pushed me back. That's it."

"Where are your groceries?" Jace chin-nodded to Caleb's empty hands.

He shifted his feet. "I just needed to...get to the restroom, boss. I'll get 'em in a few minutes."

Jace chewed on the end of a straw, seemingly without a care in the world. Caleb knew that wasn't true, but the boss didn't generally enjoy Caleb's jokes and jabs. "After you put your stuff away, I need you to get on over to the calf barn. Nelson brought in a sick cow, and I need your opinion."

Caleb couldn't keep the groan inside this time, and he hated how it made him sound. "All right," he said. "But didn't you hire a new vet?"

"Sure did." Jace pushed away from the pillar. "But they don't start until Monday."

And Caleb knew Jace wouldn't call them in on Saturday, even if the whole herd went down. Well, maybe if the whole herd went down. But the foreman tried to make sure everyone got a weekend off every now and then, something Caleb appreciated.

Jace looked out over the horizon. "See you in the barn in a few minutes."

Caleb nodded and practically ran to his cabin, which sat fourth in the line. He used to share with a cowboy named Landon Edmunds, but Landon had gotten married a year ago and moved to the horse ranch he'd bought in Utah. For some reason, Jace hadn't assigned anyone else to live with Caleb, and Caleb actually liked the solitude in the evenings.

He washed his hands and took a moment to crank the space heater all the way to high. Then he dialed Nathan, hoping his brother was home from school.

"Little bro," Nathan said by way of greeting.

"You're only older by three minutes," Caleb said, his usual response, a grin crossing his face. He and Nathan had gotten into *so much trouble* growing up. Caleb had loved every minute of sneaking through dark fields, climbing over locked fences, and kissing pretty girls. It had been his brother who'd pulled him from the wreckage of his life, made him promise never to drink again, ordered him to get clean and get happy.

Caleb had accomplished a couple of those things, and most of the time he thought he was happy. Certainly happier than he had been, especially since he'd been going to church.

"What's goin' on?" Nathan asked, and Caleb noted the western slant in his voice, despite the fact that his brother lived in Michigan now. Caleb had often teased him that he must like a long, torturous winter, because Michigan wasn't much better than northern-central Montana.

Now that Caleb had his brother on the phone, he didn't know how to bring up Holly. He swallowed, the words still not there.

"Caleb?"

"I ran into someone today," he started.

"Sounds intriguing." A baby started crying in the background, and Nathan murmured something Caleb couldn't catch. He used the distraction to organize his next statement.

*It was Holly Gray. Whatever happened with you guys?* He rolled his eyes. Nathan would see through that in two seconds flat. He'd tease Caleb relentlessly if he let on that he was interested in Holly.

He almost scoffed. How could he be interested in Holly? The very idea was ridiculous—especially because she thought he was Nathan.

"Sorry about that," Nathan said. "Eddie's tired."

"I know how he feels." Caleb wiped his hand over his face, reminding himself he still needed to get over to the calf barn and then get his groceries from the administration lodge. The thought of his standard dinner—a banana-bologna sandwich with butter and mayo—made his mouth water.

"So you met someone today."

"Not really met," Caleb said. "I mean, I already know who she is. She grew up with us, but she left town for a while."

"Oh, it's a woman."

Caleb could practically see Nathan as he leaned back, that wide smile on his face. He was sure his next words would wipe it away.

"Well, who is it?" Nathan asked.

"It's Holly Gray."

Nathan made a low, hissing sound. "Holly Gray. Wow."

"She thought I was you."

"And?"

"And she said we should get caught up."

Nathan laughed, but it held undertones of bitterness. "She really is a special kind of crazy."

Caleb's throat felt sticky. "You never told me what happened with you guys."

"She's crazy," Nathan said again, and Caleb was grateful he didn't bring up *why* Caleb didn't know what had happened. "And once I figured it out, I broke it off with her."

"So…if I…I mean, if she and I…." Caleb exhaled, wishing he'd never called Nathan.

"Are you saying you want to go out with her?"

"No," Caleb said. "Not go out with her. Maybe just hang out or something. She seemed fun."

"She was fun," Nathan said. "I'll give her that."

"So you'd be okay with it. If we hung out."

Nathan laughed again, this time the sound much more natural. "Caleb, you're twenty-six-years old. And I'm married and have a son. You can do whatever you want with Holly Gray."

"I don't want to do anything with Holly Gray. Just hang out or whatever."

"Right," Nathan said sarcastically. "I know you, Caleb. And Holly is gorgeous. I can put two and two together."

"I—I haven't dated since Robin," Caleb said. It was what he didn't say that would've blown everything wide open. *I haven't dated since I stopped drinking. Haven't had to tell anyone about that. I haven't gone out since the accident. Haven't had to tell a woman why I limp, why my bones know when it's about to snow.*

"Believe me, I know," Nathan said. "Mom talks to me about it every week when I call. She's just about to sacrifice a goat or something to get you married." Caleb snorted. "I mean, I get it. She's worried about you."

"I'm just fine," Caleb said.

"Are you? Keepin' your promise?"

"Yes, Nathan." Caleb hated feeling like he was the younger, irresponsible brother. He knew Nathan meant well, and it did touch Caleb's heart that someone cared about him enough to ask the hard questions. "So…Holly?"

Nathan chuckled. "Always with the one-track mind. Remember that year you wanted to build a tree house? You were out there every day, all summer long."

"It wouldn't have taken as long if you'd have helped," Caleb said.

"Yeah, the floor probably wouldn't have fallen through the first time you walked on it either." Nathan chuckled, and Caleb joined in. "Just don't say I didn't warn you about Holly," Nathan said.

Caleb let his grin spread. "I like a woman who's a little crazy."

———

Holly skipped church on Sunday because she simply couldn't bear to show her face there—yet. Truth was, she hadn't shown her face in church for a while. She used Sundays to work or study—or catch up on much-needed sleep.

She'd prayed and prayed for a different ending with Nathan, and when she didn't get it, her faith had grown cold, turned hard, sunk to the soles of her feet. She knew her mother would ask, and she should've gone, but she couldn't.

So when she showed up at Horseshoe Home Ranch on Monday morning, she hadn't left her house except to get a few groceries and stop by the hardware store for a new showerhead. The one in her rental didn't spray hard enough, and she had a *lot* of hair to wash and condition every day.

Her new boss, the ranch's foreman, Jace Lovell, had said there would be a formal staff meeting in the administration lodge. She'd worried needlessly about being able to find it, because as she came down the snow-packed road and eased her truck around the bend, the lodge lived up to its name. It stood two-stories tall and proud, and had obviously been the homestead in the past.

The present homestead sat a hundred yards west of the

lodge, twice as big and twice as impressive. The road divided the current homestead from the rest of the ranch buildings, including two horse stables, two large equipment sheds, several other barns and outbuildings, and a long row of cowboy cabins.

Her heart stutter-stepped, but she tamed it back to its normal pulse. She was well-qualified for this job. She had a bachelor's degree in veterinarian medicine, and she was only here for eight months to get the required hours she needed to apply for graduate school in large animal care.

*Eight months,* she repeated like a mantra. She could live in Gold Valley for eight months, drive all the way out to Horseshoe Home for eight months, weather anything for eight months.

She got out of her truck and tugged down the hem of her coat. Not wanting to spend any more time outside than necessary, she hurried toward the administration lodge and up the steps. No one else seemed to be around, and though the sky was barely lighter than twilight, she hadn't gotten the time wrong. The sun just took forever to rise in February.

She entered the building, breathing in with relief at the blast of heated air.

"Holly." Jace waved from a doorway opposite of her. "In here."

She wove through a maze of desks, which gradually gave way to long tables with chairs positioned down the sides where the cowboys obviously ate, as a bottle of ketchup still sat in the middle of one table. Her step was sure and strong as she approached the room. Men's voice filtered out to her, and she froze.

She wasn't early. If anything, they'd been waiting for her. She should've known cowboys got up at the crack of dawn, and an eight-thirty staff meeting meant morning chores were already completed.

Taking a deep breath, she took the few remaining steps to the doorway, a wider swatch of the room coming into view with each passing second. This room held circular tables, all filled with men wearing cowboy hats. Some also wore leather jackets, while some only had on long-sleeved shirts. They all wore jeans and cowboy boots, and the masculine scent of horse and sweat and cologne assaulted her.

"Boys," Jace started and the room quieted. "This is our new veterinarian, Holly Gray."

Twenty-five pairs of eyes landed on her, and she was extremely glad she'd worn the fitted, olive-colored coat. Not that it offered much protection from the gazes of all those men. At least she'd fit in because she wore jeans and boots too.

"Good morning," she said.

"She'll be running our medical clinic this spring, and I expect you all to show her how we do things here at Horseshoe Home."

One of the men leaned toward another and whispered something. They both smiled and chuckled, and Holly found somewhere else to look. She'd been up at the crack of dawn too, thank you very much. Not a lock of hair sat out of place, and her makeup was flawless. Maybe not the most practical when she'd be working with animals all day, but she wanted the cowboys to take her seriously.

Her eyes landed on Nathan Chamberlain, and her face split into a grin. When he'd broken off their engagement five years ago, he'd had two years of college left. Maybe he'd been as devastated as she'd been. Maybe he'd quit school and had been working at Horseshoe Home all this time.

She'd left town, unable to stay in such a small space with him. It had taken her a lot longer than eight months, but she'd let him go. But looking at him now, she wasn't so sure she'd made the right decision. He looked away from her as Jace said she could go ahead and sit. Somehow she got her feet to move, got her knees to bend, got herself out of the spotlight.

# CHAPTER 2

$\mathcal{H}$olly wasn't sure of all the tasks Jace assigned to his cowhands. She'd worked at a horse boarding farm in Vermont for the last two years, but the facility wan't nearly as large as a cattle ranch. A few stables, a barn, and a lot of land. She'd cared for, fed, and maintained up to forty horses on the site.

But horses weren't enough, and the amount of hours she needed to apply for a graduate program seemed impossible.

*Eight months*, she told herself as Jace talked about shoeing, and salting, and setting fence lines. He assigned men to fix windmills, and shovel stalls, and feed cows.

"Gloria is serving lunch today," he said. "At the homestead, from eleven to two. Make sure you tell her thank you."

"Yes, sir," some of the boys murmured, and Holly wondered if she was invited to lunch too. Jace hadn't given her an assignment yet—not that she'd heard anyway. Her mind had been churning with the sheer size of this place compared to Steeple Ridge Farm, where she'd worked previously. Heck, this ranch probably had more than forty horses alone, not to mention the cattle.

"Caleb," Jace said. "You're with me and Holly today."

She looked around for Caleb, the name tickling her memory, but no one stood out. The men started talking as they set about their tasks. Several came over to her and tipped their hats, saying, "Ma'am," as they passed. She noticed more than one who let their eyes linger on hers.

Holly smiled and nodded back, her self-consciousness nearly paralyzing until the room emptied. Only then did she breathe a sigh of relief. Then she turned around and came face-to-face with Nathan.

"Nathan," she said, her heart practically beating against her teeth.

He shook his head. "I'm not Nathan. I tried to tell you yesterday."

"This is Caleb," Jace said. "He's my back-up when I need time off or my baby is sick. He's the smartest of us all, too, with a degree in agricultural sciences."

Holly reeled, her feet stumbling backward. "Caleb?"

"Nathan and I are twins," he said. "Remember?" His chocolately brown eyes burned with pure fire, and she couldn't believe she'd been so stupid. Of course Nathan wouldn't be working a ranch. He'd never liked the outdoors much—which was the exact reason she'd gone into veterinarian medicine. Nathan didn't like animals either.

"Of course I remember," she said. "I just…forgot." That

sounded better than saying she'd only ever had eyes for Nathan, despite the fact that he and Caleb were identical twins, despite the fact that she'd been best friends with their little sister growing up.

"Sure, forgot." Caleb rolled his eyes as he walked past her. "Well, we're startin' in the calf barn this morning. We have a situation out there."

She hurried to follow him, baffled at his reaction to her statement about forgetting about him. "A situation?"

"Caleb thinks one of our yearlings has pneumonia," Jace said.

"He does," Caleb said, glancing back at the other man. "He's got all the symptoms."

"Just one cow?" Holly asked.

"Just the one," Jace said. "One of my boys pulled 'im out of the herd on Saturday because he was coughing. Wouldn't eat anything either."

"His temperature is up," Caleb added as he opened the door and stepped into the winter like the cold didn't touch him. "And not just 'cause he's happy to see me." He grinned at his lame joke and skipped down the steps. "He's totally depressed and just sort of lies around," he added.

"So he's not happy to see you at all," Holly teased, unsure of where the words had come from.

Caleb paused and looked at her from underneath his dark brown cowboy hat. "He's *totally sick* of me." A grin made him even more handsome than she thought possible.

"Okay," Jace said. "That's enough."

Caleb threw a laugh into the sky, and Holly wanted to

catch it, hold onto it, hear it when she lay down to sleep at night. Her feelings came with surprise, and she had to remind herself that Caleb was not Nathan, even if they looked exactly alike, right down to the way Caleb's eyes crinkled in the corners when he smiled and the smattering of freckles across his cheeks and nose.

"C'mon, boss," Caleb said. "Better to laugh than cry, right?" He tilted his head to the side as he approached the barn. "I think the yearling's bawling, though. He must be related to you." He ducked into the barn with a chuckle as Holly tried to figure out the joke.

She glanced at Jace, who shrugged one shoulder. "I guess I cry more than I laugh? I don't know. I don't get that one." He entered the barn too, leaving Holly a moment to offer up a spontaneous prayer.

*Let me figure out this situation*, she thought. She hadn't actually worked with cows as much as she had horses. *One of the reasons you're here*, she told herself as she stepped through the doorway, realizing she'd thought to ask for divine help even though she wasn't sure God heard her.

At least it wasn't as cold inside the barn, but the smell that assaulted her certainly didn't improve her mood or settle her writhing stomach.

---

Caleb waited against the fence where he'd quarantined the yearling, his insides in pure turmoil.

*I forgot.*

Caleb had always been the more forgettable twin, and he knew it. Knew it and hated it. Everyone gravitated toward Nathan growing up, because Nathan was smart, Nathan was athletic, Nathan was popular.

Caleb, though he looked just like Nathan, didn't play football. Didn't take advanced classes. Didn't care what others thought about him. He'd turned to jokes and pranks to get people—sometimes his own parents—to notice him.

His head ached and he squeezed his eyes closed to get the pain to go away. Didn't work, and he felt hot and steamed from the way his thoughts rotated furiously in his head. He hadn't even been able to come up with a decent joke because of his irritation with Holly.

*I forgot.*

As if being mistaken for Nathan wasn't enough, now he was being completely forgotten by people he'd grown up with.

He huffed as she neared, and he nodded toward the black yearling, who moaned pitifully. "See the discharge? Doesn't that look like pneumonia to you?"

She cast him a look that held more nerves than challenge, something he remembered her having. "I'll check it out." She eased into the pen and went about checking the calf. "His temperature is elevated," she said, almost to herself. "Nasal discharge, but his lungs seem just—" She jumped back as the cow coughed, but the disgusted look Caleb expected didn't come.

"A cough." She met Jace's eye, once again bypassing Caleb completely. "I think it's not quite pneumonia yet."

Caleb stood straighter. "It's pneumonia."

"How many years of veterinarian school did you complete?" Holly cocked her hip, and Caleb saw that Latina fire in her eyes.

"How many years have you looked after cattle?" He didn't wait for her to answer. He turned to Jace. "It's pneumonia."

"No wonder everyone around here is sick and tired of him." Holly folded her arms as she refocused on the yearling. "It is the beginning of something. It's odd, though. Calves don't usually get pneumonia when they're this old," she said. "I should check the whole herd."

"Can you get him on antibiotics?" Jace asked.

"Yes." Holly climbed the fence this time, and Jace and Caleb moved back to give her room to jump down. "But he should be kept separate from the herd for at least a few weeks." She pulled her phone from her coat pocket and tapped on it. "Where do you—oh, there's only one animal pharmacy in town." She frowned at the screen. "I should've known," she muttered. When she looked up, Caleb couldn't see a hint of her unhappiness. "That'll be ready in a couple of hours. I guess I'll—"

The barn door slamming into the wall cut her off. Caleb turned toward the door at the same time everyone else did. Ty stood there, his chest heaving.

"Boss, you better come quick."

Jace didn't ask a single question before striding down the aisle, Caleb right behind him. "Talk," Jace barked the closer he got.

"There are more sick cows."

An hour later, Caleb once again stood against a fence, this one with a mixture of mud and snow packed in every direction around it. His breath billowed before him and the mud on his jeans had caked and dried, making his pants twice as heavy and infinitely colder.

Jace exhaled loudly as he joined Caleb. "I'll need you to get down to town and get the medicine."

"No problem."

"Take Holly with you."

Caleb felt like Jace had thrown a bucket of water in his face. "What? Why?"

"She can get more medicine than you can, for starters."

"Starters?"

Jace squared his shoulders and turned toward Caleb. "I need you to go with her so she can load her boxes into her truck, and your truck." He spoke slower than usual, and that was saying something.

Caleb squinted at him. "Are you tellin' me she's moving up here?"

"She has half a herd of cows to look after," he said.

"So that's a yes."

"Well, she can't be drivin' back and forth in the winter." Jace started to move away, and Caleb nearly went down on a slick spot of snow in his haste to follow him.

"Why not?" he asked. "People do it all the time, and she has a truck." He didn't want to admit he liked that little fact about her. He didn't know many women who drove a truck, certainly none who had curves like Holly's.

"I need her up here, and she just got to town. She's livin' with her parents." Jace leveled his gaze at him, and Caleb shrank back a step. "So she doesn't have much and hasn't unpacked hardly anything. I need you to go help her load up, get the medicine, and get back up here."

Caleb let Jace go this time, numb inside and out—and not because of the weather.

# CHAPTER 3

By the time Caleb made it home, hours had passed since the sun had set. His muscles felt like gelatin, and his patience lingered at the very bottom of the deepest hole on the ranch. What he really wanted—a drink—he couldn't have.

But Holly was moved in, and as many cows as possible had been started on their antibiotics, and Caleb had completely missed lunch at Gloria's. And he despised missing lunch at Gloria's.

He stomped into his kitchen, dinner way past due as well, and pulled out the jar of peanut butter and a box of graham crackers. He made several cracker sandwiches and then poured himself a tall glass of milk to dunk them in.

Even after finishing half the box's worth of sandwiches, his hunger wasn't satiated. He wished he had some French fries and a chocolate shake to dip them in. He could make one of those—he always went to town the day he ran out of ice cream—but he knew he couldn't get fresh potatoes as crisp as he liked them. He'd tried once, on another disastrous day like today, when what he craved he actually didn't want in his life. Food was an easier addiction to manage, he knew. No one had senselessly run off the road because they'd eaten too much pie.

He kicked off his ruined boots, stripped off his muddy pants, and barely made it to bed before collapsing. Exhaustion consumed his muscles, but he couldn't fall asleep, because Holly also dominated his thoughts.

She'd been nice about the drive down into Gold Valley. Grateful for his help the whole time he schlepped boxes from her house down the non-salted sidewalk to his truck and then hers. She'd worked as hard as any of the cowhands —as hard as him—as they administered medicine to stubborn cattle.

He'd delivered her to her cabin door only two down from his, and she'd wiped her bangs off her forehead and given him a weary smile. "Thank you, Caleb."

Her voice—sweet and filled with gratitude and like a lullaby—still echoed in his head. He shoved it out and finally found sleep.

The next morning, he was up, showered, dressed, and standing at the stove when someone knocked on his cabin door. "Just me," Jace said as he entered the cabin.

Caleb's mood fell about ten floors, but he gestured the foreman into the kitchen with the rubber spatula he was using to make his scrambled eggs. He added a healthy scoop of cottage cheese to the eggs, along with some salt and pepper, mixing everything up nice.

"I brought you some leftovers from lunch yesterday," Jace said, setting a container on the counter next to Caleb.

"Thanks." He slid the eggs onto a plate and dumped more cottage cheese on top of them, then he reached for the salsa he'd whipped together himself that morning. A layer of salsa went on top of the eggs and cottage cheese and Caleb collected the barbeque chips from the pantry.

"What are you doing?" Jace asked.

"Eating breakfast." Caleb put his plate on the table and pointed at the stove. "Want me to make you some eggs?"

Jace pinched the corner of the potato chip bag and lifted it. "I'm intrigued."

Caleb snatched the chips away from him, ripped open the bag and used a particularly large chip to scoop up a bite of egg, cottage cheese, and salsa. He stuck the massive bite in his mouth, the flavors exploding against his tongue. "It's good," he said around the food. He swallowed and added, "No silverware to wash either." He flashed a grin as Jace grimaced.

He managed to eat the entire plate of eggs before he let his anxiety about Jace being in his cabin take over. After all, the foreman never made six-thirty a.m. house calls, not to Caleb.

"So what can I do for you, boss?" Caleb got up from the table and washed his plate. He stacked it in the dish drainer before he realized that Jace hadn't said anything.

"I'm not gonna like what you have to say, am I?" Caleb faced Jace.

"I need you to help Holly with the herd."

"Get Ty to do it. He liked her the first time he saw her in the grocery store." So had Caleb, but he wasn't going to tell Jace that. Didn't want to admit he'd called his brother and asked to hang out with Holly. Both of them knew "hang out" meant "date," and a rush of embarrassment filled him. All that had changed once he'd learned Holly had "forgotten" about him—and that she was now working at the ranch.

"I need you to do it," Jace said. "You're the one with the degree."

"In agricultural sciences," Caleb said. "Nothing medical about that."

Jace thumped Caleb on the chest. "It's your job to make sure the herd is raised to become the best beef possible. They won't make it there if they've all got pneumonia."

"The good doctor doesn't seem to think they have pneumonia." Caleb made a face.

"You don't have to like her to work with her."

Caleb sighed and his strong shoulders lowered. "It's not that I don't like her."

Jace grinned and leaned close. "I know that," he said. "Anyone with one good eye can see you're interested in her."

"I am not." Caleb took several steps through the kitchen and living room to get his hat. He mashed it on his head. "So I'm stuck with her for the foreseeable future, is that it?"

Jace joined him in the living room. "She'll only be here for eight months, Caleb." He twisted the doorknob and turned to leave. "Oh, morning, Holly. Right on time." He tipped his hat and continued across the porch and down the steps, leaving Caleb to wonder how much of the conversation Holly had heard through the door.

From the blazing fire in her dark eyes, she'd heard *some*thing.

———

Holly's heart hammered against her ribcage. *Stuck with her* looped through her ears, getting louder with every repetition.

Caleb stared at her like she'd stunned him, and she strode forward on somewhat shaky legs. Once inside his cabin, she slammed the door behind her and faced him with clenched fists. "Stuck with me?"

With her words, he seemed to recover from the stupor he'd fallen into. "Don't worry," he said. "You can just *forget about me* once you're done here." He reached for his coat, his eyes sliding dangerously up.

"Don't roll your eyes at me," she said, stepping right into his path so he couldn't leave. "For the record, I don't want to work with you either."

He glared down at her, and she wished she had eight more inches of height so she could look him straight into the eye. "Good thing you'll only be here for eight months then." He reached behind her for the doorknob and pulled open the door.

She pushed it closed again and took a deep breath. "Okay, so maybe we got off on the wrong foot."

"The one where you thought I was Nathan and were *so happy* to see me again? That one?" Caleb settled all his weight on his back leg and folded his arms. "You know he's married, right? Married and living in Michigan. They have a baby boy."

Holly knew, but his words still hit her like a punch in the gut. "I know." She didn't have to tell him she'd texted around to her old high school friends—including Katie, Caleb's little sister—to find out.

"I'm not interested in being your second choice." Caleb's voice sounded strangled and strangely muted. He opened the door again and left. This time she let him go, watching him walk away and noting the distinct limp in his right leg. She wondered what had happened to him and if she could find that out with a few texts too.

"Of course you can," she muttered to herself as she made to follow him. "This is Gold Valley after all."

The ground that had been churned up yesterday afternoon had refrozen, and Holly's boots crunched against it as she followed Caleb to the pens where they'd put the sick cattle. He was already inside, already checking the eyes of one cow, his breath rising like a cloud above him.

She climbed the fence and joined him. "I'm sorry," she said.

"This better be the right foot," he said without looking at her. "I only have two."

She reached out and put her gloved hand on his arm. "I knew you weren't Nathan at the grocery store."

That got him to stop and look at her. His beautiful brown eyes searched hers, but she wasn't sure if he found what he was looking for. "I—I guess maybe I still had some hope for me and Nathan." She gave a strained laugh. "Which is really stupid. He made it really clear we wouldn't get a second chance." That was why she'd left town the very next day.

"Are you still in love with him?"

"What?" Holly started laughing, this time the sound genuine and clear and free. "No. No, I got over Nathan a long time ago."

Caleb cocked his head at her, much the same way her childhood dog had when she'd asked him a question. Verne was a golden retriever, and very smart. A lot like Caleb, actually.

Shaking her head to clear it of the fact that she'd just compared a man to a dog, she said, "I didn't mean that I had hope for us."

"You say a lot of things you don't mean." Caleb stepped around one cow and started checking another. "You're very confusing."

Holly got to work too, because she was confused herself. She *had* gotten over Nathan. She *wasn't* in love with him. So why had she reacted the way she had at the grocery store? Why did her heart leap and skip when she saw Caleb? Was she forever doomed to be plagued by the Chamberlain brothers?

# CHAPTER 4

*M*ontana in February wasn't to be trifled with, and Holly worked quickly to keep herself warm. "What happened to your leg?" she asked as they moved down the row of cows together.

Caleb cast her a cutting look from the corner of his eye. "That's a bit personal."

She nodded though he bent behind another cow. "Fair enough," she said. "Just thought maybe I'd *milk* this opportunity to get to know you better."

He straightened and met her eye, a strange sense of wonder in his. "You realize these are beef cattle, right? We're not a dairy farm." His lips twitched and those eyes sparkled like amber. "Though it is always a good idea to turn the *udder* cheek and *mooove* on."

A giggle burst from her mouth, one she couldn't contain even if she'd wanted to. His deeper laugh twined with hers, and Holly thought for the first time that maybe she'd not only make it through the next eight months, but that she could enjoy them.

The lowing of cattle drowned out their laughter, and Holly tucked a strand of hair back inside her hat and got back to work. She pretended not to notice when she caught Caleb watching her, and she made sure to say exactly what she meant when she spoke to him. But administering eye drops and antibiotics didn't require a lot of talking, a perk of working with animals over people.

Holly knew she wasn't particularly good at communicating with others. It was why she didn't call her mom on weekends, why every relationship she'd ever had had ended, why she'd already confused Caleb to the point where they'd had to start over.

And he was right—he only had one more foot. She wasn't sure why she cared, but as she clapped her hands together and a cloud of dirt floated into the air, she knew she did. She cared what Caleb thought of her. Cared that he didn't want to work with her. Cared about it all.

Her mom had once told her that a person spent time on what they cared about, and the more Holly did just that, the more she believed her mom's adage to be true.

"Lunchtime," a cowboy called, and Holly poked her head up above the yearlings. Her stomach roared, and she wondered if she'd get fed lunch everyday. She hoped so, because she wasn't terribly skilled in the culinary arts.

Jace met her at the fence line. "Nelson made lunch. He's the best in the kitchen, and I believe it's chicken enchiladas today."

Holly grinned as she ducked under the rails. "Is lunch provided every day?"

"Not every day." Jace stepped toward the administration lodge. "But most days, especially in the winter. You got the leftovers I sent over this morning?"

"Yes." She grinned. "Thank you. Your wife is very nice."

"Good to hear it." Jace studied the ground as a smile crossed his face. "She doesn't normally leave the house before nine—or even get up before six."

"Not a morning person?"

"Not even an afternoon person." Jace chuckled and Holly joined him as they mounted the steps. "Oh, and I need Caleb out with the healthy herd, so I'm gonna move Ty over to help you this afternoon."

Holly's heart dropped to her boots and it didn't rebound back the way she thought it would. "Ty?"

"He was with Caleb at the grocery store? When you ran into him on Saturday?" Jace cocked one eyebrow at her, and she wondered how the man knew everything.

"Yes, I know who Ty is." Holly reached the porch and faced Jace. "I'm just wondering if you really need Caleb."

Jace studied her for two heartbeats before his mask cracked. "I can see why he likes you." He moved past her and into the building, leaving her out in the cold in more ways than one.

———

Caleb didn't normally go down to the valley in the middle of the week. He worked too much for such luxuries, for one. And number two, he didn't usually like to subject himself to his mother's scrutiny if he didn't have to. But after a day like the one he'd had on the ranch—with mud, and sick cattle, and the phantoms of Holly's laughter in his head—he needed an escape.

Jace had pulled him into the mechanical shed in the afternoon, but he hadn't been able to escape his thoughts of Holly. And when Ty had shown up on Caleb's porch, blabbering about Holly this, and Holly that, and did Caleb get a chance to experience how good Holly smelled?, Caleb had decided on the spot to go see what his mother had made for dinner.

His headlights cut a path through the darkness as he rounded the last bend and exited the canyon. He automatically glanced to the left, to the area reinforced with cement barriers along the side of the road. Without them, his truck would've gone all the way down into the river.

*Thank you,* he sent up, the prayer he offered every time he passed this spot. He hoped he would have the same peace and gratitude once he finished dinner with his parents.

Their windows sat in darkness when he pulled up to his childhood home, but he had a key and the garage code. He knew they weren't home, though, because his mom was nothing if not routined, and she always turned on the outdoor lights. He was actually surprised she hadn't done it before leaving, especially if she knew they wouldn't be home before dark.

He got out and approached the house, opting for the front door with his key. "Mom?" he called as he entered. He flipped on lights as he went, but his mom and dad clearly weren't home. He opened the fridge and pulled out a container of what looked like his mother's creamy chicken noodle soup.

As it heated, he texted his sister Katie, who lived in town above the hair salon where she worked. *Do you know where Mom and Dad are?*

*My place. I permed Mom's hair this afternoon and Dad ordered pizza.* A few seconds after the first text came in, Katie added, *You want to come over?*

Caleb pulled the soup from the microwave and stuck it back in the fridge. He much preferred pizza to soup, and with Katie as a buffer, his mother wouldn't be able to question him as relentlessly as she usually did.

Several minutes later, he climbed the steps to Katie's apartment, the smell of pepperoni and pizza sauce lingering in the stairwell. He knocked at the same time he entered and found his dad parked on the couch, a basketball game on the television in front of him.

"Hey, Dad." Caleb sank onto the couch next to him. "How's the construction business?"

"Cold."

Caleb chuckled with his dad before getting up and going into Katie's kitchen to get himself some dinner. He placed a kiss on his mom's forehead, the smell of ammonia and perming solution so strong his stomach twisted.

"Hey, Katie." He gave her a quick squeeze and started

back toward the living room, thinking maybe he'd only stay for a half an hour or so.

"Hey," Katie said as she removed another roller from their mother's hair. "Don't run off before I can talk to you." She met his eye, and a sibling secret passed between them. She raised her eyebrows and Caleb suspected that she knew about Holly.

"Yeah, sure," he said. *Of course she knows about Holly,* Caleb thought as he moved back to the couch. *They were best friends in high school.*

He settled onto the end of the couch, suddenly fearful that Nathan had told Katie about Caleb's phone call. The three of them had been close growing up, and it wouldn't surprise him if Nathan had talked to Katie about Caleb's schoolboy crush, maybe even asked her to keep an eye on Caleb and make sure he was okay.

He ate his pizza, but didn't taste a single bite. A real shame for someone who loved food as much as Caleb did. Finally, the hair was done, and the game ended, and his parents left. Katie closed the door behind them and then leaned into it, a wicked smile on her face.

"What?" Caleb asked. He wouldn't be the one to bring up Holly. Everything was about plausible deniability, especially when it came to women.

"Holly texted," Katie started. "Holly Gray, remember her?"

Caleb's mind raced. He wasn't sure if he should say "Yeah, your best friend in high school, right?" or "Sure, wasn't she Nathan's fiancé?"

He released a breath he'd been holding and dismissed both options. "Yeah, she's the new vet out at Horseshoe Home. What about her?"

Katie skipped toward him. "She asked about you," she sing-songed.

Caleb scoffed though his heart soared. "She did not."

Katie flopped onto the couch next to him and leaned into his chest as he put his arm around her shoulders. "She did. She wanted to know if you're always so grumpy."

Caleb blinked, not sure he'd heard his sister correctly. "What?"

"She said—"

"I've been nothing but nice to her," he interrupted. "I am *not* grumpy."

Katie tilted her head back and grinned up at him. "She said something about you rolling your eyes and barking orders and—"

"I'm at *work*," he said. "I was just giving directions. There was no barking involved."

"And the eye rolling?"

"So maybe I rolled my eyes—*once*—when she said she'd forgotten about me."

The teasing sparkle in Katie's eyes went out. "She said she forgot about you?"

"She sure did." Caleb's chest pinched painfully. "So I get a free pass on that eyeroll." He eyed her, glancing down and then back to her eyes. "And you need more girlfriends."

"What does that mean?"

"It means then you'll have someone besides me to gossip

about." He stood, his right ankle aching a bit from the stationary position he'd been in.

"Oh, believe me," Katie said through a giggle. "I get plenty of that at the salon."

He spun back to her, eyes wide and pulse running wild. "You haven't said anything about me to any of your clients, have you?"

"Caleb." She shoved him in the chest. "Of course not."

He shrugged into his coat. "Good. I don't need everyone in town thinking I'm grumpy." He scoffed as he opened the door.

"That's not all she said," Katie said, the mocking quality back in her voice.

Caleb turned slowly, not sure he wanted to know what else Holly had said about him. He leaned against the door to give relief to the lingering ache in his ankle. "Oh?"

"She asked if you had a girlfriend." Katie danced away from him, her phone clutched in her hand. "I haven't answered her yet."

Caleb's stomach warmed and his chest expanded. He knew he hadn't imagined the fire between him and Holly, he just wasn't sure if it would burn him or not. "Good," he growled. "Don't. None of your business."

"Are you saying you have a girlfriend I don't know about?" Katie's eyes rounded and a bit of hurt leaked into them.

"Maybe."

She lifted her chin. "What's her name?"

The air whooshed out of Caleb's lungs. "Fine, I don't have a girlfriend. But it's not your place to tell Holly that."

"Why not?"

"Because," Caleb said. "We're not in junior high anymore. We're adults. If she wants to know if I have a girlfriend, she should ask me."

Katie blinked at him once, twice, three times before looking at her phone. "I'll tell her that."

Caleb nodded, pushed his cowboy hat lower on his head, and left his sister's apartment, glad that was over and done. Still, a thrill that Holly had been asking about him stayed with him all the way back to the ranch.

All the way up his front steps, where a figure emerged from the bench just to the left of the front door. He paused, taking in the curve of Holly's hips, the curled tips of her hair. "Hey," he said.

"So." She stepped fully into the light, and that dangerous fire danced in her eyes again. "Since we're not in junior high anymore, I'm wondering if you have a girlfriend."

# CHAPTER 5

$\mathcal{C}$aleb glanced around, desperately hoping no one
was passing by, that no one had heard her. He kept
his eyes locked on hers as he opened the front door and
ushered her in. Once the door was closed, he said, "You
could've just come in. How long you been out there?" He
tossed his keys onto the table next to the front door and
slipped his arms out of his coat. "It's cold."

"Not long," she said. "I know how long it takes to drive
up to the ranch from the valley." She cocked one glorious
hip and put her hand on it. His fingers twitched toward her,
but he pushed them into his pocket instead. "Are you going
to answer my question?"

His throat went dry, his brain and his heart battling with
each other. He was attracted to Holly, no doubt about that.
But Nathan's words about her being crazy circled in his
mind like vultures, and he didn't know how to handle such
a straightforward woman either.

"I don't have a girlfriend," he managed to say. "You hungry?"

"It's almost ten o'clock at night."

"I don't see how the time is relevant to hunger." He hurried into the kitchen and pulled a package of cheddar from the fridge. "You like cheese and apples?" He grabbed a Granny Smith from the bowl next to the microwave and started slicing.

"I'm not hungry," Holly said.

"You said I was grumpy," he blurted. As a flush rose through his neck, he grabbed a slice of apple and layered it between two pieces of cheese, quickly stuffing the whole thing in his mouth so he wouldn't say something else he couldn't take back.

"You asked for a different job so you wouldn't have to work with me."

He swallowed before he was all the way finished chewing, a corner of the apple dragging against his throat. "You said we could start over." He threw his hands into the air. "I'm all out of feet, Holly."

She stalked one step, two steps, closer. "Well, I have two more."

Caleb stared at her, complete puzzlement running through him. "I don't understand you."

A smile quirked her very full lips, which seemed way too pink for so late at night. He leaned closer to her. Was she wearing lip gloss at ten p.m.?

"I do aim to be mysterious."

He chuckled. "Mysterious I understand. You're downright—" He cut himself off before he could say *crazy*, but he had a feeling Holly heard it anyway.

"I'm downright what?" She came closer, trapping him in the kitchen.

He reached for more cheese and more apples, unsure of how to answer. "You know what's better than just cheese and apples? Cheese and apples with peanut butter and crackers." He lunged for the cupboard and pulled out the peanut butter. In his haste, he knocked his knuckles against the cracker box and it thunked onto the floor.

Holly stepped into his personal space, rendering him still. She removed the butter knife from his hand and set it on the counter very deliberately, ignoring the graham crackers he loved. He looked at her hand as it fell back to her side, then he lifted his eyes to hers. She stood so close, he could smell the soft, creamy scent of her skin and the feminine floral quality of her hair. Her hair, which he wanted to fist in his fingers as he kissed her. His gaze dropped to her lips, but he yanked them back to her eyes.

"I'm downright what?" she asked again.

"Beautiful," he murmured, not even sure when he'd thought the word let alone told his mouth to say it. He couldn't take a full breath, and he simultaneously wanted to pull Holly closer and get as far from her as possible. His brain spun, and his heart whirred, and he had no idea what to say or do next.

Robin had never made him feel like this before—no one had—and he didn't know how to navigate such treacherous terrain. He'd had casual relationships over the years, women he looked for at the summer dances and made sure he spun with before he and the other cowboys went back to the ranch. Nothing beyond that. And those weren't real relationships anyway. Just him having fun on a summer night.

But now, looking at Holly, Caleb wondered if it was time to get a little more serious. He swallowed, but his tongue stuck to the roof of his mouth. "Could you step back?" he asked, his voice barely more than breath. If she didn't, he was worried he'd slip his hands around her waist, bring her closer, and kiss her until that lip gloss was gone.

She complied, but she took her sweet time doing so, a flirty smile on her face. Holly bent to retrieve his crackers and set the box upright on the counter next to the peanut butter. "Well, I better go." She walked backward slowly, her dark eyes inviting him to come with her.

He matched her step for step, the thread between them so strong he couldn't have resisted even if he'd tried. And he didn't want to try.

Holly leaned into the door, and he put his hand on it so she couldn't open it and leave quite yet. "How about you come over for dinner tomorrow night?" he asked.

"Do you actually know how to cook?"

"Didn't you see me wield that knife? I had that apple sliced in seconds flat." He leaned down, satisfied when she inhaled and closed her eyes. "I'm good in the kitchen, I promise." His voice had never sounded so husky, and he worried he was revealing too much, too soon. What that exactly was, he wasn't sure, because his emotions tumbled like clothes in a dryer.

"Okay," she said.

"And I'll talk to Jace in the morning," Caleb added. "You should know I didn't mind working with you this morning."

"Could you step back?" she whispered.

Caleb did, the sparks between them practically lighting up the whole cabin. "Sorry."

"I should go."

"Yeah." He pulled off his hat and ran his hand through his hair.

She turned and cracked the door. "Oh, and Caleb? I'm allergic to eggs. Not sure if you remember the time I threw up all over your deck because Katie made those cookies and didn't use an egg replacement. I don't want to repeat that."

Caleb chuckled as the memory flooded his mind. "I do remember that."

She ducked out the doorway, and he moved to lean into it so he could watch her until the night swallowed her. When he finally shut out the winter cold, he moved around his cabin, cleaning up and getting ready for bed in a daze. Had he just asked Holly out?

Definitely not. He'd asked her to stay *in* with him. And she said yes.

He grinned. She said yes.

———

By the time Holly arrived in the sick pens the next morning, the cowboys were already singing as they slung hay in the feeding troughs. She glanced around, trying to find Caleb— no, Jace. She needed to find *Jace*.

Luckily, he exited the barn next to the pens and made a beeline toward her. "Mornin'." He turned back the way he'd come. "Caleb's waitin' for you inside. He's got some special feed he wants to try." He didn't seem strange or weird or like he knew Caleb would be cooking for her that evening. He moved away, calling to another cowboy as he went.

Holly stepped into the barn, wishing the warmth didn't come with such a strong smell attached to it. She passed the tack room and a couple of empty horse stalls on her way to the room where she'd stocked the medical supplies.

She found Caleb there, muttering to himself, his head bent over a notebook on the folding table in front of him. He swiped off his dark brown hat to reveal sandy hair that curled over his ears and along his neck. She wondered why he hadn't had his sister cut his hair, and then wondered if he liked keeping it a bit longer.

"What have you got there?" She walked the few steps to him and glanced at his papers at the same time he glanced at her.

"Hey there." He flashed her a smile and pointed with his pencil eraser. "There are about a hundred cows who've lost weight. I'm putting together some special feed to get them back to full health quicker."

She looked at the numbers cascading down the edge of the paper. "How do you know these cows have lost weight?"

He tapped his pencil against the notebook. "I can tell by lookin' at 'em."

"Really?" She cocked her head to the side. "I mean—I don't doubt you, it just seems…pretty amazing."

"I work with them all day, every day." Caleb settled his weight on his left leg and sighed. "Jace said I could put together a special feed for them, including the antibiotics, and you and I could monitor them over the next couple of weeks." A sliver of a smile curled his lips. "'Course we have to monitor all the cattle, but I want to try this with the group I've targeted."

"So we can't just throw them some hay." The time it would take to feed even a hundred head individually seemed impossible.

"Nope." Caleb scooped up his notebook and stuck the pencil in a jar in the corner of the table. "But Jace said we can build a separate trough, and herd the cattle into the holding pen where we brand in the spring."

Fear struck Holly right in the chest. "Build a separate trough?" She had never picked up a hammer for more than putting a nail in the wall to hang a picture. She had never been able to make two pieces of anything line up, much to her mother's dismay that Holly couldn't even sew a pillowcase.

Caleb edged closer to her in the already tight space, the energy between them blooming into electricity in less time than it took to inhale. "I put a homemade spaghetti sauce in the crock pot this morning." He reached up and tucked an errant curl behind her ear. "No eggs in spaghetti and meatballs, yeah?" The smile he graced her with was filled with gentleness and kindness and only increased her desire to get to know him better.

"Sometimes there's eggs in meatballs," she said.

"I soaked some bread in milk and used that as a binder." Caleb's fingers drifted down the side of her face, trailed along her arm, and landed against hers. Everywhere he touched, even against her coat danced with fire, and she curled her fingers around his and tugged him a half-step closer.

"Did you know it's Valentine's Day?"

His other hand crashed against hers as panic reared across his face. "It's what?"

"It's Valentine's Day." She giggled. "I knew you didn't know. Don't worry about it." Still, something inside her withered a little bit. She'd reasoned before falling asleep last night that he hadn't asked her simply because it was Valentine's Day—that he probably didn't even know. But her hopeless romantic notions remained.

"I would've made a dessert or something," he said.

"There are eggs in most desserts." Holly shook her hair over her shoulders and gazed up at him. "Besides, I think you'd be the best dessert." She bit her lip, not quite sure what she meant by that.

Caleb searched her face too, obviously confused as well. "I'll round up some chocolate or something. That doesn't have eggs, does it?"

She leaned into him. "How about I bring the dessert?"

"Sounds great." He leaned down as if he'd kiss her, but

approaching footsteps had him jumping back and releasing her hands.

"Caleb," a man called only moments before poking his head into the room. By then, Holly had her arms full of antibiotics. "Oh, hey." Ty volleyed his gaze from Caleb to Holly and back, pure delight entering his eyes. "I didn't mean to interrupt."

"Sure you didn't." Caleb smacked him in the chest with the notebook. "Nothin' to interrupt anyhow." He glanced at Holly, the desire in his eyes as hot as ever. "We're just getting the meds for the yearlings and prolonging the moment before we have to go out into the subzero temperatures."

Holly groaned on cue and flipped up the collar of her coat. "Better get to it." She moved past Caleb and squeezed past Ty. "Apparently we have to build a new feeding trough too."

"Yeah, that's what I came to talk to you about," Ty said. "Jace sent me over to help with that. Said he didn't want it to take too long since he needs you in a meeting this afternoon."

Behind her, Caleb exhaled heavily. "I forgot about that meeting."

"Something with agriculture and new feed laws."

Holly kept walking, so she didn't hear Caleb's response. He caught up to her just as she nudged the door with her elbow. "Dinner will be a bit delayed tonight."

She didn't break her stride and matched her voice to be as quiet as his. "We can do it another night if you want."

"No," he said quickly. "It'll just be closer to…seven than six."

She nodded, wondering if relationships were frowned upon at Horseshoe Home—or if Caleb just wanted to keep theirs under wraps for now.

She mis-stepped when she realized she'd just thought of herself being in a *relationship* with Caleb Chamberlain. Fear morphed into terror, which formed into horror. She kept her hands and mind busy—and her mouth closed—as Caleb and Ty built the trough and she administered medicine to the appropriate cattle.

Just before lunchtime, Caleb opened the gate and began herding the selected cattle into the branding pen. He called and slapped the cattle, the same way Ty did, and once the proper cows were corralled, Caleb clapped his gloved hands together and drew a deep breath. His strong shoulders lifted and squared, which caused a smile of appreciation to lift Holly's lips.

"Time for lunch," he announced. "I could eat a horse."

Ty's boisterous laughter filled the air, and Caleb joined him as they made for the administration lodge. Holly followed behind, reminding herself that just because Caleb had asked her to dinner didn't mean they'd do everything together. She still had a job to do on the ranch, and he had a lot of friends here. She couldn't expect him to drop everything and spend his lunch hour with her.

Upon entering the administration lodge, pink and purple hearts greeted them. Someone on the ranch obviously knew it was Valentine's Day, and Holly smiled as Ty pulled down a heart and crumpled it in his fist.

Caleb cast her a glance, tipped his hat, and entered the kitchen. She kept her smile concealed and went to get her own lunch, her stomach practically eating itself inside out. In the kitchen, she found a long table set up with the largest pan of enchiladas she'd ever seen. A big bowl of salad. And a tall, clear jug filled with pink lemonade. Cowboys moved down both sides of the table, chattering and laughing. With a tremor of unease, she joined the line.

The men were cordial, but none of them spoke to her. With her plate full, she exited the kitchen and paused, looking for a spot where she could sit, rest, eat, relax. She didn't see Caleb, though she spotted Ty at the end of a table several paces away.

She put her plate down and slid into a seat, wondering where Caleb had got to. Maybe she could take her plate back to her cabin, eat her lunch without so many bass voices in her ears. When she saw a couple cowboys duck out the door with their plates, she picked up her food and went to follow them.

A couple of men down the hall to her right caught her attention. She froze as she realized it was Caleb and Jace, and they seemed to be arguing. Holly ducked her head and hurried away, not wanting to get caught listening where she shouldn't. Maybe she'd been like that once. Maybe she'd once always needed to know the latest gossip. But she was different now.

Besides, she'd find out that evening when she went to Caleb's for dinner.

———

Caleb stared at Jace, the excuse he needed simply not there. He didn't want to tell the foreman that he'd asked Holly to eat dinner with him after only one day—a half a day—of working with her. She'd been in his life for five days, and he couldn't understand his feelings, let alone explain them to the tall, tough foreman.

Jace waited, a knowing look in his eye, his arms folded. "So there's no reason you can't babysit, like you promised you would."

"There's a reason," Caleb said.

"I'm dyin' to hear it." He pushed his cowboy hat back and smoothed his hair. "You know Belle hasn't left the ranch since Christmas, right? If I tell her we can't go…." He clucked his tongue and shook his head. "Have you been around my wife when she's mad?"

Caleb had, and he didn't want to repeat that, thank you very much. "Fine," he growled. "What time do I need to be over to your place?"

"As soon as the meeting finishes and you can shower," he said. "Our reservation isn't until eight, and that should be plenty of time." Jace glanced over Caleb's shoulder and back to him. "Belle will have Tucker in bed. You know that, right? You just have to sit there and watch TV until we get home." He shrugged and his voice went up in pitch when he added, "You could have someone over as long as you're quiet."

Caleb flinched like he'd had cold water splashed in his face. "Have someone over? Who would I have over?" He narrowed his eyes and searched for an answer on Jace's face. He couldn't.

"I don't know. Maybe whoever you made that spaghetti sauce for."

"I didn't—"

"Please. I can smell it from here," Jace said. "It's my favorite thing on the planet." He smiled, his normally sharp and iron eyes softening. "So you bring on over that pot of spaghetti and meatballs, and you enjoy your…meal, and you leave me some." He clapped his hand on Caleb's shoulder. "And I'll text you when we're comin' back up the canyon, so you can make sure you're alone when we get back." Jace didn't wait for a confirmation, just turned and walked into his office, leaning out the doorway. "Tryin' to fool me is like tryin' to sneak sunrise past a rooster." He grinned and shut the door behind him, the final word on the subject.

Caleb turned back to the open area, where cowboys ate and laughed. So he needed to move his Valentine's Day dinner to his boss's house. Big deal. But somehow, it felt like a big deal.

For one, he wouldn't be able to kiss Holly in someone else's cabin. He'd never be able to take her there again, create a special moment between them when they needed it. He scrubbed his too-long hair at the base of his neck, trying to dismiss his romantic ideas. But they wouldn't go.

He glanced around to find Holly, and only a few seconds passed before he noticed she wasn't there. He found Ty, who had Caleb's plate of food next to him. "You see which way Holly Gray went?"

Ty pointed his fork toward the door, and Caleb swept his plate away with, "See you later." He ignored Ty's whoop as he hurried back into the cold, his stomach still pinching with want of food but his heart urging him to hurry to the sixth cabin in the line.

# CHAPTER 6

Holly almost choked when someone practically beat down her front door with their bare hands. "Holly!" a man called, and it sounded dangerously like Caleb.

Surely he wouldn't be yelling her name while standing on her front porch. She jumped up from the couch, almost planting her red sauced plate against her chest. She yanked open the door and sure enough, there stood the most handsome cowboy in the state of Montana.

"What are you doing here?" she demanded, the old fire she tried to keep dormant flaring up.

"I needed somewhere quiet to eat." He held a full plate of food—more than she thought possible a single person could even eat—and wore a grin the size of Texas.

She leaned into her doorway. "I believe you have an empty cabin." She nodded to her left. "Right there."

He glanced over to his cabin. "I needed to talk to you." He tipped his hat toward the space behind her. "Can I come in?"

"It's a free country." She stepped out of the doorway and swiped her empty plate from the coffee table in front of her couch. The door closing behind Caleb, the door trapping them together in her cabin, made her blood feel like someone had dropped a bucket of nails into her veins.

He groaned as he sat on her couch and started eating. She took her trash into the kitchen and stayed there, not quite trusting herself to sit next to him on the couch. "So what's so important that you couldn't text me?"

"Number one." He pointed his plastic fork in her direction. "I don't have your number. So I need to get that. Number two." He wiped his mouth with a napkin, and she wanted to trace her fingers across his clean-shaven jaw. "It wasn't that important. I just wanted to eat lunch with you, and you'd disappeared from the administration lodge."

Happiness had never felt this warm. Holly had forgotten how good it felt to receive a compliment, how nice it was to have a man look at her like she was worth something. Sure, she'd dated on and off since leaving Gold Valley, but nothing serious, and nothing as fiery as what she felt with Caleb after only one encounter.

*You don't need a man to have worth*, she told herself, something she'd believed for the first two dozen years of her life. And she knew she didn't, but she couldn't help feeling warm and fuzzy from the sly way Caleb watched her.

"So you have nothing to say?" she asked.

He stuck the last bite of his enchilada in his mouth and chewed, those eyes almost concealed beneath the brim of his cowboy hat. Still, she could feel the weight of them on her; feel it deep down in her soul.

"It's about our dinner tonight." He took a swig of his lemonade and sighed. "So since it's Valentine's Day, Jace and his wife Belle are goin' down to dinner. Apparently, I volunteered to babysit."

Holly stared at him, the words registering as English in her ears, but they didn't quite make sense. "What?"

"It's more like house-sitting," he said. "Their baby, Tucker, will already be in bed. But if we want to eat dinner together, it'll have to happen at Jace's house."

Every internal organ inside her torso reshuffled herself. "The big one on the end, right?"

A sparkle teased her from across the room. "They're leaving at seven. You can come on by any time after that." He picked up his fork and started eating again.

She watched him for another moment. "I don't see how you're gonna be able to eat again today," she said as he polished off another enchilada.

He stood up and laughed, grabbed his plate, and stalked closer to her. "This ain't nothing, sunshine. I'll eat again after my chores and before my shower." He forked a bite of salad into his mouth and grimaced. "This needs ketchup."

"Ketchup?" She watched, aghast, as he opened her fridge, pulled out a bottle of ketchup, and squirted some on his lettuce, carrots, croutons, and ranch dressing. Her stomach revolted against the enchilada she'd consumed. "I feel like I'm gonna throw up."

"You don't have to watch." He wiped a large leaf of lettuce through a glob of ketchup and stuck it into his mouth. "Mm, it's good." He stabbed another piece and held it toward her. "Try it."

She shook her head and pressed her lips together.

"Come on," he teased, advancing toward her with that salad-ketchup fork.

"Caleb," she warned. "Don't take another step."

He did, and then another, a sexy smile combining with a dangerous chuckle that had her nerve-endings quivering. "One little bite," he coached.

"If you even get that close to me, I will—"

He paused and tilted his head a couple of inches to the right. "You'll what?"

Her eyes flickered to his mouth and back to the fork. "I don't know. But it won't be pretty."

Caleb lunged at her, but Holly dodged, a squeal erupting from her mouth. "Caleb!" She knocked his hand away from her face, and the fork went flying. Ketchup splattered the wall and the cupboard, but that fact disappeared behind the warmth of Caleb's hands on her waist, the vibrating of his chest against hers as he laughed. Though she wasn't sure how she felt, or why this relationship seemed like it was on fast-forward, she laughed with him and hung onto his shoulders as he turned with her as if they were dancing in her kitchen.

They quieted, and she laid her cheek against his chest,

the steady bump of his pulse bringing comfort to a place in her life that had been tumultuous for far too long. For the first time since Nathan had broken off their engagements, Holly felt like she could find love again.

She cleared her throat, eternally glad Caleb could not read her thoughts, and stepped away from him. "You're gonna have to clean that up." She gave the ketchup splatter a dirty glare.

"Only if you say you're coming to Jace's tonight. Did I mention I made spaghetti sauce for dinner tonight?" He picked up the washcloth in her sink and turned on the water. "From scratch. It's my mother's recipe, and well, she might kill me if she knew I was feedin' it to pretty women." He started cleaning up the offending ketchup.

"So this is something you do a lot, then?"

He dropped the washcloth like it had caught fire and turned to stare at her. A dark edge entered his eyes. "Not for a while, no."

"Define a while."

"Well, let's see." He exhaled. "I'd say it's been about five years since I've eaten dinner with a woman."

She gave him a coy smile. "You have a mother and a sister."

He grinned. "That I do. I guess I meant to say it's been five years since I've eaten dinner with a beautiful woman I'm interested in."

Though the temperature in her kitchen seemed suffocating, she managed to say, "You should say what you mean."

He ducked his chin to his chest, a quiet chortle meeting

her ears. "Yes, I should." He lifted his gaze back to hers. "I called Nathan, that day you hugged me in the grocery store? I had to ask him what had happened with you guys, because…." He swallowed noticeably, and the depth of fear in his eyes seemed bottomless.

Holly wasn't sure why he was afraid, but everything inside her had gone cold at what Nathan might have told Caleb about her. "I don't need to know," she said quickly. "You should go."

Caleb blinked, confusion erasing the fear. "What?"

"I don't want to know what your brother said about me." She didn't know her voice could sound so arctic, but she couldn't help it.

"He didn't say…." He trailed off when his phone rang. He checked it, his shoulders drooping. "It's Jace. I have to take it."

"Take it." She gestured toward the front door, still icy inside.

"You haven't said you'll come tonight," he said over the blaring of his phone.

"I'll text you."

He answered the phone with, "Jace," his eyes never leaving hers. He covered the bottom of the phone. "You don't have my number."

"I'll get it."

He smiled and looked away. "Yes, yes, I'm here. Yes, I know I need to finish with the separated yearlings. Yes, I realize what time it is." He moved on swift feet toward the front door, where he exited, never once looking back.

Holly made it to the couch, where she sat heavily, trying to figure out how she'd gone from standing in the man's strong arms to telling him he should leave and considering not meeting him for dinner on Valentine's Day.

———

Caleb cursed himself for bringing up Nathan—something Holly definitely hadn't appreciated. He'd never seen eyes so smooth and warm and chocolatey go to rock hard and cold so fast.

Then he cursed Jace for not even allowing him to have a blasted thirty-minute lunch. So what if the yearlings hadn't had their medicine yet? He had five more hours to get it done, and with only a hundred head to get the meds out, he'd have it done within the hour. He turned back to Holly's cabin, hoping she'd have followed him out the door.

She hadn't. He mentally kicked himself again, spun away, and said, "I'll be there in five minutes, Jace." He hung up and stomped up his steps to check on the spaghetti sauce. A delicious aroma teased him from the porch, and when he entered the house, he thought it a real shame Holly couldn't come here. Sure, she could eat at Jace's, but the scent was part of the magic of homemade spaghetti sauce.

He stirred the sauce, wondering how in the world she was going to get his cell phone number. His ankle throbbed —a storm was coming in—as his frustration rose, and he tossed the wooden spoon in the sink before heading back out to deal with ornery cattle and even more irritable—and irritating—men.

His phone chimed, and he glanced at it. *I'll be there.*

The grayness in the sky seemed a little bit bluer with the text. The sun broke through the clouds—something it hadn't done in a while—and a smile stole across his face. He added Holly's number to his contacts as thunder sounded overhead.

He jammed his phone in his back pocket and hurried to the sick pens. Administering feed and antibiotics would take longer in the rain, that was for sure. He found Holly and Ty there, already dishing out the laced food he'd prepared that morning. He rushed to help them, and they managed to finish just as the sky opened.

Holly yelped, peered up into the sky, and ran for the shelter of the barn. Caleb relied on his cowboy hat to keep the icy rain off his face and neck, and he flipped his collar up to keep the wind from snaking inside as he finished forking extra hay into the pens.

His phone went off, and so did Ty's next to him. Caleb also heard several others which belonged to cowboys who worked nearby.

"Callin' us in," Ty said.

Caleb tipped his face toward the sky and offered a prayer of gratitude that Jace was a reasonable man, that the rain could get him out of the cold until the meeting started. His stomach soured at the thought of the agriculture meeting. Maybe the storm would make watching the live feed impossible.

"Let me tell Holly," Caleb said as Ty started toward the administration lodge.

"Sure," Ty said. "You go tell Holly."

"What does that mean?"

"It means Jace has her number too." Ty laughed as he slopped away through the slush and mud.

Caleb ducked into the barn anyway, just to be sure. It wasn't because he wanted to be alone with Holly. No sirree. After all, she was coming to dinner that night. His feet froze to the barn floor when he realized maybe Jace and Belle wouldn't go down to dinner if the weather was bad.

Maybe he could still have his romantic dinner with Holly in his own cabin, the tantalizing smell of tomato sauce the perfect backdrop for the perfect kiss….

"Caleb?"

He blinked away the fantasy and came face-to-face with Tom, Jace's brother. "You okay? I think Jace called everyone in."

"Oh, right. Yeah. He did." Caleb glanced around, wishing he wasn't fantasizing so much about Holly. He didn't trust himself not to go off the deep end if something serious went south with a woman. And there he was, thinking everything would go wrong with Holly.

*Why wouldn't it?* he asked himself, his familiar inadequacies resurfacing. A horrible thought entered his mind—maybe Holly only liked him because of her past with Nathan.

A vicious cycle started in his mind, one where he played second fiddle to Nathan, the way he always did. Then where he had something great with Holly only to be ruined by his trust issues, first with himself and then with her.

"Hey, you all right?" Tom waved his hand in front of Caleb's face.

He jolted away from his thoughts, a physical reaction that he wished was as easy to do mentally and emotionally. "Did you see a woman in here?"

"Dark hair?"

"How many women are out on the ranch?"

Tom chuckled. "Yeah, she was here. She ran for it as soon as the call came in."

So she was on Jace's list. Foolishness tripped through Caleb. Of course she was. She worked at the ranch now—as hard as any of the cowboys too.

"Okay, great. Thanks Tom. What are you doing out here?"

"Just looking after the horses before I head in. Mari will ask about them, and I want to be able to tell her they were safe in their stalls during the storm." Tom flashed him a brief smile and went about his work.

Caleb left the barn to a brutal wind that blew the rain sideways, making the drops more like needles as he hurried toward the administration lodge. It wasn't his job to check the weather, so he didn't know if this would last the rest of the day or blow over in a few minutes. He hoped for the former, hoped the WiFi would go out, hoped hoped hoped for a storm that would ground everything on the ranch to a screeching halt.

He usually hated that. Hated staying inside, organizing

things that didn't need to be organized. Hated going outside, where the temperatures were enough to make a man consider moving to a ranch in a far southern state. Hated waking up in the middle of the night to make sure the furnace still worked.

He burst into the administration lodge and was greeted by the scent of wet men. It smelled a lot like a wet dog, actually, and Caleb hurried to shut the door to keep the wind at bay. He maneuvered through the people and chairs to the hallway that led to Jace's office. He could get started on meeting prep and maybe sabotage the Internet connection.

He didn't touch the cables, and instead settled in the chair across from Jace's desk. He closed his eyes, reasoning that it just felt so good and he'd open them any second now and start reading the material he needed to know for the meeting. Any second now….

"Wake up, cowboy." Jace kicked his chair as he walked by. "I thought you'd have us all set up."

Caleb cleared his throat and wiped a weary hand over his face. "I was gonna get it set up. I was."

Jace jiggled the mouse and clicked, a wry smile on his face. "Did you cut the WiFi?"

"What?" Caleb swore the man could read minds. "Of course not. Is it not working?"

"Computer won't even come on."

"Is it on?"

"I was usin' it this morning."

Caleb went around the desk and peered at the black screen. He checked all the cords and said, "Try again."

The computer screen blared to life, but there was no Internet. Caleb's heart swelled in his chest. "We can watch a recording later, right?"

Jace leaned back in his chair and wiped his hands down his face. "Well, today has been a humdinger, hasn't it?"

"You're still gonna go down to dinner, aren't you?" Caleb backed up a step. "I don't want to see Belle angry."

"You're the second person I've reassured that I'm going."

"Who was the first?"

"Belle. She called as soon as the thunder started." He leaned back and closed his eyes too. "I've told her two more times. I think if we can't go, she'll eat me for dinner." He chuckled, but it sounded strained.

"What's the weather supposed to be like?"

"It's a fast-moving storm, and it'll blow over in a couple of hours."

Caleb watched his boss, saw the exhaustion in the lines of his face. "Maybe we can just take a nap until then," he suggested.

"Can't," Jace said. "It's payroll this week, and I could get it done in a couple of hours."

"So can I go take a nap?"

Jace laughed and opened his eyes. They seemed a bit blurred, like he couldn't focus for a few seconds. "Nice try, Caleb. I need you to organize the afternoon chores and split them up so we can get five hours worth of work done in only two. As soon as that storm blows over, we can get the men back out there."

Caleb groaned and flopped back into the chair. "Really, Jace?"

"Really, Caleb. We have animals to feed and take care of. When you're the foreman—"

Caleb scoffed, effectively silencing Jace. "Why is that strange to you?"

"Because, Jace." Caleb ran his fingers down the sides of his face, his beard already growing back. He hated shaving almost as much as he disliked winter. "I'm never gonna leave Horseshoe Home, didn't you know?"

Jace heard the sarcasm in his voice, but he didn't react beyond a slight head tilt. "Who told you that?"

"No one," Caleb mumbled.

"You don't want a ranch of your own?"

"No." Caleb shook his head vehemently. "No, I don't. I like the cowboy life just fine." He sighed and supported his head with his hands, his elbows poking out to the sides. "I love the summers in those fields, and the stream in the upper fields, and the smell of freshly mown hay."

"Those are all summertime ranching duties."

"I like ranching in the summertime."

"You like branding?"

"I don't hate it as much as I do feeding the herd during a snowstorm."

Jace shuffled some papers around on his desk and inhaled sharply. "You should check out some ranches in Texas. Tom has contacts down there. No snow."

"What makes you think I'm not happy here?"

"Nothing," Jace said, still moving those blasted papers around like they needed to be in a different position.

"Good," Caleb said as he stood. "Because I am perfectly happy here. I like Horseshoe Home, and believe it or not, I like Montana."

"You'll never be a foreman if you stay here."

"I don't want to be a foreman." Caleb opened the door and smiled over his shoulder. "They're too stuffy." He ducked out of the room amidst Jace's protest.

Caleb scampered around the kitchen, garlic-buttering bread and tossing a package of drink mix and a pile of paper products in a box. He couldn't take everything over at seven—Jace didn't care if Caleb had a date in his living room, but the unspoken word was that Belle would. So Caleb got everything as ready as possible, the delicious smell of garlic and tomatoes hanging heavy around him as he put on his coat.

At Jace's house, Tucker was not in bed as promised. Belle bounced the one-year-old on her hip while Jace brooded from the kitchen. "Oh, Caleb, thank goodness." Belle passed him the little boy like he'd know what to do with him and spun back to Jace. "We can go now."

"Wait," Caleb cried. "You said he'd be in bed."

"He's almost ready," Belle said over the boy's low wails. "Just keep bouncing him until he wears himself out. His diaper's been changed and he has a sippy cup in the fridge you can give him when you put him down."

Caleb had a whole new understanding of why Jace looked so tired all the time. He pinned the foreman with a death glare as he helped his wife put on her coat. He shrugged, half an apologetic look on his face before they opened the door and left. All of Caleb's ideas for what this evening would look like left with them.

He focused on the little boy, who had Belle's bright eyes and Jace's dark hair. He seemed to be leaking from every hole in his head, and Caleb smiled at him. "Oh, come on now, Tucker. It's not so bad." He plucked a baby wipe from the tub on the kitchen table and wiped the boy's face. "You want a treat? What kind of treats does your mom have around here?" He opened a cupboard and found a box of crackers. "Bingo."

He fed Tucker snacks until he stopped sniffling, then he pulled the sippy cup out of the fridge. "You want this?"

Tucker reached for it and Caleb pulled it back, laughing at the boy's smile. "You have to go to sleep now, okay? I have this woman coming over, and I still have to go get the bread and get it browned up before she gets here." He started down the hall and Tucker whined again.

"Nope," Caleb said. "No crying. You've had a treat, and you have your milk, and…." He watched as Tucker's eyes blinked closed slowly and opened again. "You're tired. Time for sleeping." He entered the bedroom and put Tucker in his crib, tucking him in tight as the boy started drinking his milk.

He left, pulling the door closed behind him. He paused, taking a deep breath and listening for the sound of any distress. Nothing. A smile bloomed on his face, but it only lasted a few seconds. He really did need to finish dinner. He strode toward the front door and pulled it open.

"Oh, whoa." Caleb fell back before he could ram into Holly, who stood on the porch, a pan of something clutched in her hands.

———

Holly blinked at the glorious sight of Caleb standing in the doorway, the soft light from the house framing him angelically.

"Come in, come in." Caleb stepped back. "So Tucker was still awake when I got here, and I just got him down, so dinner's not quite ready yet."

Holly entered the house, noting how much bigger and nicer the foreman's cabin was than hers. "So these are brownies made with applesauce instead of eggs."

Caleb eyed them like they were made of sawdust. "Sounds great. I have to run back to my cabin. Can you stay with Tucker in case he wakes up?"

She nodded and he ducked out the door, leaving her alone with her thoughts. She'd heard him cooing to the little boy, talking to him like he was a real person who understood. Though she hadn't been able to see him, he'd somehow claimed another piece of her heart with his ability to get fussy babies to bed.

She admired the pictures of Jace, Belle, and Tucker while she waited for Caleb to return. When he did, the smell that came with him made her stomach twist with hunger. "There's no ketchup in there, is there?" She eyed the box he carried.

He chuckled and held the door open with his foot. "No, but can you come grab this?"

She did and took the items into the kitchen while he bent and picked up a crock pot. "I hope you like pasta, because I have enough to feed the whole ranch."

"Who doesn't like pasta?"

He set the pot down on the counter with a thunk. "My feelings exactly." He grinned down at her, and time seemed to slow into thick strands she could grab and hold onto. "So how did you get my number?" He pulled a loaf of bread from the box and split it open. It already had butter smeared on it, and he opened Jace's cupboards like he'd cooked there before.

She wondered if he had, then immediately frowned. Why did she care if he'd cooked for another woman? Of course he had. Caleb Chamberlain wasn't hurting in the looks department, nor the muscles area, nor the charm counter.

*You already asked him that besides,* she chastised herself. Still, she wasn't sure why she had this tug-of-war going on inside. She liked him, and normally she didn't question that. But this time…this time, something about liking *him* specifically needled at her.

"Your sister," she said, dismissing her thoughts for now.

He tapped a button on the oven to turn it on. "Ah, now I know who the traitor is." The grin he wore when he turned back to her could've lit a whole farm of Christmas trees. Holly couldn't help but return the gesture.

"I've been in touch with her," she said. "It's nice to have a friend in town."

Caleb watched her for a breath past comfortable. "I understand that. You keep in touch with anyone else from high school?" He busied himself with setting out the plates and ripping open a package of drink mix.

"A few people," she said. "Some still live here, some don't."

"Where did you live before this?"

"Vermont," she said, finally comfortable with him in such close proximity.

"Ah, another one who must like the torture of winter." He stirred the punch with a chuckle in his voice.

"I didn't see you move away from Montana," she teased.

"Nope."

"So you've never left?"

Caleb twisted toward her and searched for something on her face. He apparently found it, because he said, "No." He turned back, his earlier joviality dimmed. He stuck the bread in the oven, set a timer, and faced her. "Well, I think we're almost ready."

"Know any hunger jokes?" She stuck her hands in her back pockets and rocked on her heels. "Because I'm starving."

"Does a knock-knock joke count as a joke?"

Holly shrugged. "Depends on how lame it is."

He cleared his throat, an adorable flush climbing into his cheeks. "Okay, well, knock knock."

"Who's there?"

"Hungry clock."

"Hungry clock who?"

"Hungry clock who went back four seconds." The sparkle in his eye made her smile. "Get it? Went back for seconds?"

She giggled, the sound growing and changing into a full laugh. "I get it."

He inhaled and exhaled, the first sign of nerves from him and all of Holly's anxiety came roaring back. She searched for something to say, some joke about anything, but her mind came up blank.

Caleb spun back to the crock pot. "So this is my mother's tomato sauce recipe."

She stepped next to him, enjoying the warmth that leaked from his body and flitted across her skin. "What's in it?"

"I can't tell you that." He spoke with such seriousness, she glanced up at him. He gazed at the pot of spaghetti. "It's a family secret."

"I didn't know the Chamberlain twins could cook. Nathan—" She cut herself off, the awkwardness between them mushrooming until Caleb moved away from her.

He opened the oven though the timer hadn't gone off. "Nathan doesn't cook." He left it at that, and all at once,

Holly understood why she'd been going back and forth about beginning a relationship with Caleb.

She wasn't sure if she really liked him or if the memory of her relationship with Nathan was the basis for her admiration of this look-alike twin.

Tears sprang to her eyes and she ducked her head before the kitchen lights could show Caleb what she didn't want him to see.

"Katie is pretty useless in the kitchen, too." Caleb closed the oven and walked toward her. She kept her face away, unsure of the emotions she wore in her eyes and the tightness of her mouth. "I told you I was good in the kitchen." His strong hands landed on her shoulders and stroked down her arms, eliciting a spark when his skin touched hers.

She had an idea that he'd be good everywhere. Anywhere. She sighed involuntarily, wanting to enjoy her precious alone-time with him. She was attracted to him, and her past with Nathan had nothing to do with that.

At least that was what she told herself over and over. And over.

# CHAPTER 8

Holly woke several days later and stuck the last of her leftover spaghetti in the microwave to heat it for breakfast. As it was Sunday, and she wasn't a ranch hand, she had the day off. Her plans included first the pasta. Second, a hot bath. Third, a movie marathon with caramel popcorn somewhere in there.

She whistled as she padded around the kitchen and started a pot of coffee, her thoughts lingering on the Valentine's Day date with Caleb, the secret hand-holding in the barn when they were alone, the way he watched her from across the corral.

She'd been wrestling with herself over why her attraction to Caleb seemed through the roof from the moment they'd met. She honestly had thought he was Nathan, and she'd been thrilled to see him. She hated that after everything that had happened, everything Nathan had said, she'd still felt a flicker of hope that day in the grocery store.

With everything she'd learned since then, with all she felt for the other Chamberlain brother, she needed some time to figure things out. Time to listen to her own feelings and learn how to trust them.

Her phone sounded at the same time the coffee pot started to bubble. She reached for the phone and grinned when she saw Caleb's name on the screen. That euphoria faded as she read his invitation to church.

*Church?* she typed out. Before she could second-guess herself, she sent him the text.

*I got the whole day off, which never happens,* he responded. *I thought maybe we could go to church together, take a little walk around town or something.*

She squinted at the phone, sure he hadn't sent the right message. *It's twenty below zero.*

*I gotta get off this ranch.*

She didn't. She was perfectly content to stay in her cabin all day, the fire roaring as she lay in bed and caught up on her reading. She wasn't taking any classes right now, but she had plenty to read about cattle and horses. She'd need to test into the program, and she couldn't let even a week go by without reviewing or reading something.

She glanced up, letting her gaze wander around the sparsely furnished cabin. *Eight months.* She was leaving Gold Valley in eight months. Was it even worth starting a relationship with Caleb?

"Too late," she muttered. "You probably shouldn't have held his hand if you didn't want to start something with him." Oh, they'd definitely already started something. Now it was a matter of how it would end.

Holly's heart cartwheeled in her chest. She couldn't handle another devastating break-up. It was why, after Nathan, she'd never gotten serious with another man.

But this was just going to church with the guy. That wasn't serious. So she typed, *Sure, church. What time is that?* and pulled her spaghetti out of the microwave.

———

Caleb's heart felt tied to helium balloons as he trotted down his steps and hurried down the row to Holly's. She was right. A walk around town in temperatures like these was out of the question. What else could he do then to keep her with him?

Things hadn't gotten terribly romantic at Jace's, despite his best efforts to woo Holly with delicious food and buttery carbs. Sure, she let him hold her hand, and she'd curled into him on the couch as they talked, but a kiss was completely out of the question, and it wasn't because they were in the wrong location. But a tension had existed between them, one he didn't know how to ease.

He knocked on the door and stuck his nearly numb fingers in his pocket. Holly opened the door a few seconds later and said, "Come in. I'm not quite ready yet."

He complied, nodding at her as he stepped into her cabin. She continued into the bedroom, calling over her shoulder, "There's coffee in the kitchen."

He poured himself a cup and opened her fridge to see if she had cream. He stared, a bit dumbfounded at the many cartons of flavored coffee creamers. He peered at them. "Hazelnut? Coconut? Chocolate?" He selected the last one, sure a mocha would make church more bearable.

He poured a healthy amount into his cup and took a sip. Delicious. He mentally added the flavored coffee creamers to his personal shopping list as Holly came out of the bedroom. He hadn't properly looked at her when she'd answered the door, but now he drank her in over the top of his coffee mug.

She wore a vintage-style dress with a narrow waist and fitted bust above a flattering, flared skirt. The black and yellow plaid accented her brown skin and dark eyes. The dress was sleeveless, but with a very wide strap over the shoulder. Caleb swallowed at the sight of her bare arms and her black high heels.

She finished fiddling with the gold necklace around her neck and looked at him. He set his mug down and growled as he prowled toward her. "You are gorgeous," he said.

A smile sprang to her face. "Thank you." She scanned him, but he wore his usual jeans and winter coat. "Are you sure we're going to church?"

"We sure are, sunshine." He slipped his hands around her waist and held her close. When she relaxed into his embrace, practically melting against him, his heart bumped irregularly. Though the situation was good, something he shouldn't be anxious about, he still felt the debilitating palpitations of panic that used to drive him to drink.

He definitely needed to go to church today. It had been several weeks since he'd been able to go, and he felt something missing in his life.

"I have a confession," she said.

"Oh, I'm not the pastor." He chuckled as he inched back to look down at her.

She swallowed, those make-upped eyes shining with an emotion he couldn't quite identify. "I haven't been to church in a long time."

His reactions warred with each other as he frowned and said, "That's okay," at the same time. "I don't get to go all the time. Ranching is seven days a week work."

"How'd you get today off?"

"The whole Valentine's Day thing." He glanced over his shoulder, trying to figure out why Holly felt like she needed to tell him she hadn't been to church in a while. He didn't know, and his usual tactic when something confused him was to change the subject. "I think you have coffee creamer problem, though the chocolate was delicious."

She followed his gaze toward the kitchen. "I don't have a problem. I can stop any time I want."

He met her eye again, found the joy within, and laughed. "I counted at least eight cartons, all different flavors."

She stepped out of his arms and collected a dress coat off the back of the couch. "Wait until Halloween. They have this pumpkin spice cream that will blow your mind."

He helped her into her coat, taking her hand in his once she was ready. He squeezed, smiling at her in his most gentle way. "Why haven't you been to church in a long time?"

She couldn't hold his gaze, something that triggered another alarm inside Caleb. For some reason, the fact that she had issues comforted Caleb. It alerted him to the fact that she wasn't perfect either, that he wasn't the only one who struggled with demons, both past and present.

"Hey, so how about I tell you why I try to go to church whenever I can?" He tugged her toward the door and she went with him, her eyes still averted. She didn't answer, so he kept right on talking. "A few years ago, I was in a car accident." His leg gave a sharp jolt of pain, as if reminding him of the incident. As if he could ever forget.

"That's how I got this limp. Broke my ankle and had surgery and lost some height in my right leg." He hurried to his truck, which he'd already started so the heater would be blowing by now. Thankfully, it was.

A slice of disappointment at the way she stayed all the way over against the passenger window made his throat close momentarily. He flipped the truck into gear, his right hand mourning the fact that it couldn't hold hers.

"Anyway," he continued as he bumped down the gravel road to the highway. "I hadn't been to church in a few years, and...." Now that the time had come to tell her about his drinking problem, he found the words simply weren't there.

He chuckled, trying to lighten the mood. "I know you think I'm the rebellious twin, and you'd be right about that." He flashed her a devilish grin he didn't feel in his soul. He forged on anyway. "After my last girlfriend, well, let's just say I looked for an escape in the bottom of a bottle." He cleared his throat and forced another laugh. "It wasn't there, in case you were wondering."

"Caleb." The soft, sensual quality of her voice enveloped Caleb in a sense of safety. That was all she said. Just his name.

"When I woke up hung over in the hospital, I knew I needed a change in my life. Church doesn't have all the answers, but I like listening to the pastor talk about the Lord, and I like how I feel when I'm there." He came around the curve, came to the spot where he sent up his prayer of gratitude. He did so again and kept that particular tidbit of information to himself for now.

"Whenever I feel like I need a drink, I remember how I feel when I'm at church." He took a deep breath like he hadn't had one since he started talking.

"How long have you been sober?" she asked.

"Goin' on four years this spring." Pride crept into his voice, and he swallowed it back. He knew it wasn't by his own will that he'd managed to stay away from the whiskey, but God who had delivered him, time and time again. "So, you feel like sharing?"

She shook her head as she clamped her lips shut, like the words might leak out if even a tiny space existed.

"It can't be that bad," he said."

"It can," she said. "You're lucky I'm here at all."

"Okay," he said, deciding to let it drop—for now. Instead he told her a joke about a pastor, a horse, and a lawyer.

# CHAPTER 9

Caleb wasn't prepared for the fallout of showing up to church with Holly Gray. Hadn't even considered it, which was pure stupidity on his part. Of course his parents would know who she was, know what had happened, and had formed opinions of her.

By the gasp and sour look on his mother's face, her opinion of Holly wasn't favorable. His dad, who usually took everything in stride, did a double-take before narrowing his eyes first at Holly and then Caleb.

Only Katie acted like a human, giving Holly a quick hug and saying hello. Next to him, his mom kept sniffing, a signal that something was seriously wrong and that Caleb would hear all about it behind closed doors.

His dad didn't even wait that long before he leaned over and said, "What is she doing here?" And not quietly either.

Every muscle in Caleb's body felt encased in cement, and he shushed his father without answering as the pastor got up to start the service. But Caleb couldn't concentrate, and for the first time since he'd returned to church, he got nothing from the sermon, nothing from the choir's song, nothing to help infuse his soul with peace.

He didn't hold Holly's hand the way he'd imagined he would. He didn't casually lift his arm over the back of the pew and pull her into his body. He didn't even so much as look at her, and by the time the song ended the meeting, Caleb wanted nothing more than to bolt out the nearest door.

He stood and followed Katie and Holly into the aisle. Holly seemed as bent on leaving as he did, but she didn't make it four steps before a mob of women descended. Maybe not a mob, but Caleb thought being approached by a group of two women constituted being accosted. And with the five swarming around Holly, his anxiety flew into the rafters.

They'd driven together, and he couldn't just leave her here, but he had no idea what to do. Every few seconds, one of the women in the mob threw him a look, and he didn't like what any of their eyes had to say.

"Caleb," his mother said, her voice set on dignified. He'd heard this tone before, as his mother was especially good at expressing her disappointment with him with a simple tone and a few choice words.

"I don't think I'll stay for dinner tonight, Ma." He leaned over and kissed her cheek. "I drove down with Holly—she works at the ranch now—and I don't think she was planning to stay."

"I'm sure she wasn't," his mom said.

"She's not invited anyway," his dad added.

"Chris," his mom admonished, but her face broadcast the same message. Holly wasn't welcome in their home.

"Well, she's not," he whispered at almost the same volume that he spoke with. "Do you know who she is?"

"Yes," Caleb clipped out, the possibility of having a real relationship with Holly disappearing into a dot on the distant horizon. How could he not have thought of this scenario? He'd called Nathan, that was why. He'd forgotten that there were always a lot of people involved in every situation.

"I know you were havin' a rough time when Nathan broke up with Holly, but—"

"Dad, I don't want to hear it." Caleb gave his dad a hard stare. "Any of it. Thanks for savin' me a seat. I'll see you later." He turned, caught Holly's eye, and nodded toward the foyer.

She acknowledged that she'd seen him and he strode away, the clipping of his cowboy boots against the wood floor too loud against his eardrums. The pastor stood in the lobby, several feet from his usual post at the doors leading outside. People streamed by him, giving him accolades and smiles. Since Caleb hadn't actually heard a word of the sermon, he wanted to avoid Dr. Pinnion if at all possible.

But the man had an eye like an eagle, and he spied Caleb before he could escape down the hall to where the community signups and Sunday school classes were held. He lifted his eyebrows along with one of his hands, and Caleb's heart sank.

He waited his turn before stepping over to the pastor. "Caleb," he said, reaching out to shake hands. "How are you? Haven't seen you in a while."

"I've been working a lot," he said. "Half our herd is down with pneumonia."

Dr. Pinnion nodded to a couple as they walked by. "So I heard."

"You did?"

"Jace told me, and then Gloria. I've been praying for Horseshoe Home."

Caleb blinked, though he shouldn't be surprised that Gloria had told the pastor and asked for prayers. She was that kind of lady—faithful and kind and a spitfire. She never missed church, and she served on the board as well.

"I saw you sitting by a woman," the pastor continued. "I didn't know her."

"She's the new vet at the ranch," he said, hating that was how he chose to explain who Holly was. But he couldn't tell anyone he was interested in being her boyfriend. "She's only been in town for a week or so. She'll only be here for eight months."

Dr. Pinnion nodded. "Well, do bring her by to meet me."

"You got it, Pastor." Caleb ducked away quickly, but he didn't go back toward the chapel, didn't want to take Holly to meet Dr. Pinnion. He just needed to get out of the church before anyone else caught his eye and wanted to know about Holly.

He headed outside and found shelter in his truck. With the engine idling, he texted Holly that he was waiting in the truck. Then he waited. And waited. She never texted him back, and as the parking lot emptied, he couldn't fathom where she'd be.

He tried calling her, but she didn't pick up. His concern now reaching epic proportions, he pulled up the curb and headed back inside. Only a couple of people lingered in the foyer; even the pastor had left. The chapel was empty except for the organist, who practiced the same few bars of a hymn over and over.

He checked down the hall, but stopped short of going in the women's restroom. His phone went off, and he checked it faster than he thought possible, his heart popping to the roof of his mouth.

But it was a text from Katie. *You should've seen Mom's face when Holly said her spaghetti sauce recipe was her favorite! Priceless.*

Caleb's lungs froze, and every breath seemed to make a cracking sound as he tried to free them from the chill encasing them. He didn't know what to text back. He couldn't fathom why Holly would mention that he'd cooked for her, that they'd spent Valentine's Day together. Why had she done that?

A flicker of anger joined the party of riotous emotions in his chest. He just needed to find her and get back up to Horseshoe Home. Then he could disappear inside his cabin and forget this day had ever happened.

————

Holly sat on the closed toilet in the restroom in the church, still trying to get her emotions under control. She'd thankfully escaped the crowd of women who'd never left Gold Valley before any of them could see her cry. Her phone had buzzed several times, and she suspected it was Caleb. She knew she only had a few more minutes before he'd probably bust down the bathroom door, and still she sniffled.

"Face it," she whispered. "There's no way you're getting out of this without him knowing you've cried." She sighed, stood, and moved out into the bathroom to look at herself in the mirror. Sure enough, her red eyes would broadcast to anyone who looked at her that she'd been crying.

She swiped on her phone and told Caleb she was in the bathroom and she'd be out in a minute. She peered at herself, the dark makeup around her eyes still intact. She paid a lot of money for the waterproof stuff, and it was nice to know it lived up to her expectations.

The thought of facing her former, now-married, high school friends had her jaw jutting out. But then she remembered how she'd used Caleb's mother—and her once future mother-in-law—to get away from the women.

"Your spaghetti sauce was so good," she'd said. She'd even put her hand on the woman's arm. Patty had looked at her hand and then her face like she was made of horse manure, and Holly realized then what a tragic mistake she'd made.

Nathan's parents obviously didn't know what had really

happened, and she shook her head. Why should they? He wasn't going to tell them their break-up was his fault. Though he and Caleb looked the same, Holly had already learned that Caleb was the more respectable twin. She'd always thought him the more rambunctious one, the one who instigated pranks and jokes, and couldn't be serious to save his life.

But she'd seen a different side of him, even in the short week she'd spent with him. Her chin shook, but she clenched her teeth together to get it to stop.

A light knock sounded on the door behind her. "Holly?" Caleb's concerned voice came through the wood.

"Just a minute." She sucked at the air and wiped under her eyes. She felt like she needed a cold washcloth to cool her flushed face. As ready as she'd ever be, she squared her shoulders and pushed out of the bathroom and into the hall.

Caleb turned from the bulletin board, his eyes appraising her all at once. "Hey." He stepped toward her, and while she'd told herself to maintain distance from him during the sermon, now she melted into his embrace. "Don't cry, sunshine," he murmured as she lost the battle against those determined tears.

She held onto him, and he held onto her, and as the moments passed, she calmed within the safety of his arms. She finally drew a deep breath and stepped back, keeping her eyes on the ground and a curtain of hair between them.

"Sorry," she muttered. "Let's go."

He linked his fingers in hers, and the way he still touched her made her feel a bit better. "I guess neither one of us thought about how my parents would react to us showing up to church together."

"I can't believe they still don't like me. It's been five years, and it wasn't even my—" She cut off, unwilling to bring up the past she'd worked so hard to forget. And surely Caleb didn't need to hear her distaste for his brother. Holly had never even told Katie the real reason she hadn't married Nathan.

Caleb studied her, and she focused on the exit, then the horizon when they walked outside. She didn't know what else to add, so she just said, "Let's just get back to the ranch."

He walked her to the passenger side of the truck and paused before opening her door. "Holly, I'm sorry." The genuine quality of his voice sent a blip of warmth through her, but everything was so mixed up now, she couldn't truly smile.

"It's—well, it is what it is, isn't it?"

"That's a lot of it's and is's." He smiled at her in that gentle way that tugged against her heart. She didn't want to fall in love with him. Her life would be infinitely easier if she just put in her hours and moved on to graduate school. She didn't need to ever see his parents again.

But when he looked at her like that…those soft edges in his eyes, the slight curve of those full lips…. She wanted to remove every barrier between them—and that included his parents and his twin.

"What did Nathan tell you about me?" She shivered, and he pulled open the door. She climbed in, thankful he already had the truck's heater blowing full-force.

He hurried around the front of the truck and got in behind the wheel. "Why do you want to know what Nathan said?" He turned toward her, his expression open and kind. She searched her memory to find a time when Nathan had looked at her like this. She couldn't find one.

"It just seems like your parents really don't like me. He must've told you guys something really awful." Her stomach writhed, and she folded her arms across her middle, almost desperate for him to start driving.

"I don't know what he told them," he said, facing the front and putting the truck in gear. "I had just broken up with my girlfriend, and well, I was pretty out of it for about a year."

She focused her attention out the window as he drove through town and past the waterfalls. She appreciated that he'd confided in her, told her about his past with drinking, told her something that made him more human, more vulnerable.

*Trust him.* The words came into her mind, but she didn't think them. She'd spent so long trusting no one and nothing —not even herself. She was starting to do that now, but it was still a process, especially with how she felt about Caleb and if it was all mixed up with her past relationship with Nathan.

"My guess is he told you I was crazy. A crazy, jealous woman who wouldn't even let him go to class by himself." Her voice sounded like she was speaking into a tin can. "An insane, delusional girlfriend who didn't trust him, who had to know where he was all the time." She faced Caleb. "Is that right?"

Caleb flicked his gaze to hers and back to the road. "He stopped at crazy."

Holly didn't know what to make of that, but maybe Nathan hadn't spent the last five years obsessing over what had gone wrong. Of course he hadn't. Holly ground her teeth together. She'd believed he was cheating on her with another woman in several of his college classes—Mel Bunting.

She'd seen texts about times they were meeting up. When she asked Nathan about them, he claimed they were study sessions. She'd tried to trust him. But he came home smelling like a woman's perfume, and his "study sessions" started happening every evening, and she found movie ticket stubs in his jacket pocket.

So she'd started following him, and sure enough, he was meeting Mel for coffee, or at the library, or in the diner. No one else but Mel. She'd never seen them exchange more than a quick hug, but when a mutual friend in Nathan's class texted and said she'd seen Mel get in Nathan's car when class had gotten out early, Holly couldn't keep explaining away his infatuation with another woman.

She'd confronted him, and everything had come out. He'd been horrified and furious that she'd followed him. Irate and unkind when she told him she'd read all of his texts. But they were supposed to be married in six months, and she didn't think he should be spending more time with a classmate than his fiancé.

He'd been cruel, using words like "paranoid," and "crazy," and "insanely jealous for no reason."

But she had reasons. Good reasons.

The best one of all was that Nathan's wife—and the mother of his one-year-old child—was Mel Bunting. When she found out they'd been married for four years, everything Holly had suspected became absolutely true.

"Doesn't matter," she said. "He didn't want to marry me, and that's what it really came down to." Because he'd broken up with her and only eleven months later was wed to Mel. Holly's engagement to Nathan had been longer than eleven months.

"I'm—I don't know what to say," Caleb said.

"Nothing to say." She inhaled and exhaled, trying to push away the poisonous thoughts and memories. "But I don't think I'll be going to church with you again."

"I think you're wrong about that."

She looked at him, and he gestured for her to slide over and sit by him. Though she had plenty of good reasons not to, she did anyway—because she wanted to.

He threaded his fingers through hers. "I think we'll sit by each other at church again," he said. "We just won't sit by my parents." His smile held a devilish hint to it, and she couldn't help but grin too.

*H*olly flirted with the idea of inviting Caleb over for coffee, but she chickened out when they pulled under the double-H arch that led to the ranch. She wanted to get in her warm bath, don her comfiest pj's, and eat a big bowl of popcorn while a romantic comedy played on TV.

He killed the engine and gazed down at her. "What are you doing for dinner?"

"I was going to make a snack and watch a movie."

One eyebrow quirked up. "You don't cook, do you?"

"Sure I do," she said. "I've been eating great all week."

"*My* spaghetti."

"It heats up nice in the microwave." She smiled and nestled closer to him. His arm lifted and he draped it around her shoulders. Holly felt very much like a teenager on her third date with the cute guy she liked, prolonging the moment before she had to go in the house in the hopes that the boy would kiss her.

"I was going to take a bath and try to forget about everything that happened this morning."

"Me too," he said. "Minus the bath." Creases appeared between his eyes. "No one should take baths. They're disgusting. You're just sitting in a tepid pool of your own filth."

She tipped her head back and laughed. "Maybe not everyone gets as dirty as cowboys do."

"I'll give you that." He squeezed her closer. "I can put something together if you want to come eat later."

She peered up at him under his cowboy hat, all her thoughts, all her reservations, disappearing in the moment. "Maybe." She pushed herself up and brushed her lips across his cheek. Just as quickly, she slid across the seat and out of the truck before she could do something else equally insane.

———

Caleb watched Holly walk down the road and up to her front door, his blood raging through his veins like class five river rapids. She'd just kissed him.

A smile rooted itself on his face, and he practically floated into his cabin. He'd forgotten what dating a beautiful woman felt like. The bounce in his step, the tune streaming from his lips, the giddiness in his gut.

The only problem—well, he had a few—was that Holly had missed with her kiss. He kept his thoughts on her as he opened the fridge and started thinking about what he could make for dinner that would entice her out into the cold and into his cabin.

"Something simple," he told himself as he reflected on that morning. He probably wouldn't have another day off for a while, and he needed this one to relax. No sense in wasting in on a high-end meal when Holly would be happy with steak and salad. He couldn't grill in the winter, so he opted for a chicken cordon bleu casserole, something that he could make now and bake off when she came over.

He chopped the chicken and the ham, shredded the Swiss, and whipped up a roux with nutmeg and cream. While the butter melted for his breadcrumb topping, he texted Holly and told her the menu.

*I've never heard of such a thing,* she responded. *It's barely lunchtime. When were you thinking?*

*Whenever you want,* he typed out. *It takes thirty minutes to melt the cheese and brown the topping. I'll stick in in when you get here, and we'll eat it while it's hot.*

*I'll let you know.*

Caleb didn't want to push her, but he wanted to know when he could see her again. He wanted a commitment— something he hadn't desired for a long time. Slightly frustrated, he removed his cowboy boots and hat, changed out of his white shirt, and decided to pass the time until Holly showed up with a nap.

His dreams featured a certain dark-haired beauty in all her curvaceous glory, but shadowy shapes flitted around in the background. His demons, or hers, or his family, he wasn't sure. But they stayed away for now, and Caleb moved in for the kiss he'd been thinking about since Valentine's Day. Maybe since the day she'd launched herself into his arms in the grocery store.

He woke just before he got his kiss, and he chuckled into sunlight streaming through his bedroom window. "Of course," he muttered to himself as he sat up. "Can't even get the kiss in my dreams."

He ran his hands over his face and checked his phone. He'd been asleep for an hour, a decent nap. With nothing to do, he thought maybe he should pick up a hobby or two. He didn't need to clean, as the ranch employed a service for the cowboys. He normally spent his evenings in the kitchen with the TV on for background noise, so he migrated into the living room and took his place on the couch. He had a tablet, and a laptop, but he didn't do much with them. He wasn't one for reading, and he didn't much care to keep up friendships with anyone he didn't see in person.

So he flipped through the channels until he landed on a documentary about World War II, and checked his phone approximately every ten seconds. It seemed like a week had passed before Holly texted, but the documentary hadn't even ended yet, so it hadn't been long.

*Whipping up a dessert, then I'll be over.*

Last week, she'd brought brownies made with applesauce instead of eggs, and Caleb had eaten at least half the pan. If chocolate was involved, he almost couldn't help himself. He wondered what she'd bring tonight, and if he'd embarrass himself by eating so much of it.

She arrived only twenty minutes later, carrying a tray of plastic cups. He ushered her into his cabin and closed the door against the sunny chill outside. "What's that about?" He eyed the cups, but couldn't tell just from looking what they contained.

"So my mom loves strawberry shortcake," she started, continuing through his living room and into the kitchen, where she set down the tray. "So last week, when I was at the grocery store, I bought these sponge cakes and a box of vanilla pudding." She glanced around the kitchen before bringing her attention back to him. "I don't have cream, but I thought maybe you did…."

"I have cream." He moved toward her. "You had fresh fruit from way last week?" It had been eight days since he'd run into her in the grocery store. Or rather, when she'd run into him. Literally.

"No, but I found a blueberry muffin mix in the back of my cupboard, and since it takes eggs to make it, I tossed out the floury part and used the blueberries." She brandished her hand toward the cups. "Thus, blueberry shortcake… with pudding." She smiled at her creation, though it just looked like vanilla pudding in a cup. Now if it were chocolate….

Caleb wanted to bring her close to him, breathe her in, kiss her until they both forgot about dessert of any kind. "Looks great," he said instead and stepped over to the oven, where he set it to preheat for the casserole. "This will only take about a half an hour." He turned back to her, stuck his hands in his pockets, and rocked up on his toes. "What do you want to do now?"

Her eyebrows shot toward her hairline and she blinked those long lashes at him.

He kicked himself mentally. "I mean, I don't really have any games or anything." He waved toward the living room. "We could watch a movie or something."

"I like movies."

"Great." Caleb exhaled and wished he'd stuffed his hat back on his head before answering the door. As it was, it hung on a hook in his bedroom, and he'd have to go hatless for now. He fumbled the remote in his haste to change the channel.

"Wait," she said. "What's this?"

"A documentary."

She sat on the far end of the couch. "You like documentaries?"

"Sure," he said as he started searching for something else. "I like to learn, but I don't like to read. College almost killed me." He couldn't find anything on TV he wanted to watch with Holly. "When I have to read for meetings and stuff now, I put it off until the last minute."

"I think I'd like to read more if I had time."

Caleb put down the remote and knelt in front of his TV cabinet to find a movie. "You probably read a lot for your classes, don't you?"

"Yeah, but it's not fiction."

He sat back on his haunches, several DVDs in his hands. "Let's see." He scanned her, enjoying the shape of her legs in her tight, dark jeans and the way her long curls trailed over the blue blouse she wore. "I think if you had time to read fiction, it would be…romance." He grinned as she blushed.

He plucked one DVD out of the bunch. "Romance it is."

"I like action movies too," she said.

"Yeah, but you like action movies *with romance*." He put the disc in the player and took his spot right next to her on the couch. "Am I right?"

She nudged him with her shoulder and he lifted his arm over her shoulder. "Maybe."

"There's no maybe about it, sunshine."

She lifted her feet and put them on the coffee table, pushing her back further into his chest. He played with a lock of her hair, his fingers brushing along her upper arm and igniting the fire in Caleb's blood to near inferno levels.

The movie started, but he couldn't focus. "So Katie mentioned that you told my mom about the spaghetti sauce."

She stiffened in his arms, and he added, "It's okay. I'm not mad or anything."

"I didn't realize how much she still disliked me. I thought it would be a compliment." Holly let her head loll against his chest. "I was wrong."

"They'll come around," he said.

"Will they?"

"Sure," Caleb said with more confidence than he felt. He wasn't sure why his parents had harbored so much animosity for Holly over such a long period of time. They'd been nothing but kind and helpful after his accident, even going so far as to look up treatment programs for him. He hadn't ended up checking into a program, but he'd moved in with his parents for three months until his leg was healed enough to come back to work on the ranch.

It wasn't like them to display such unkindness, and he frowned at the movie as he wondered what Nathan had told them about Holly. She hadn't displayed any jealousy or controlling tendencies in the short week he'd known her. Of course, he never left the ranch.

*And people change*, he thought as he remembered his own journey over the past five years. He pulled her closer and placed a kiss on her temple when she turned her face toward him. He shouldn't have done it, because all it did was remind him that he wanted to taste her lips—not her cheek, not her forehead. Her lips.

He'd just have to employ a little more patience. His stomach growled, and she giggled. "Didn't you eat lunch?" she asked.

"I did," he said. "It's been a couple of hours."

"Oh, a couple of hours." She giggled again, the sound light and deep at the same time. "I don't know how you've lasted this long." She gestured in the air, and her hand landed on his knee. He sucked in a breath before he added his chuckle to hers, a hive of bees skimming along his skin. A burn started where her hand sat on his leg, stretching in all directions.

"Hey," he said, the laughter still in his tone. "I can't help it if I like to eat." The timer on the chicken cordon bleu casserole went off, and Caleb pulled his arm away from Holly. She straightened on the couch, sliding her hand off his leg.

"Be right back." He flashed her a smile before walking into the kitchen. He took a deep breath and exhaled slowly to get himself to calm down. It had just been a long time since he'd felt anything this strong for a woman. A long time since he'd actually wanted to feel something for a woman.

And it felt good to want to share his life with someone. Felt real good.

Caleb pulled the casserole out of the oven, admiring the crispy brown breadcrumbs. "This looks fantastic," he called. He pulled cream from the fridge and stuck his beaters in the electric mixer. Even through the noise of whipping the cream, he noticed Holly lean against the fridge. Noticed the way she watched him with her arms crossed across her chest. Noticed the admiration in her eyes.

He warmed under her scrutiny, and when the cream reached soft peaks, he switched off the beaters. "We can eat on real plates today," he said. "You want to grab them out of that cupboard?" He pointed toward the cupboard behind him. "I'll grab the silverware. Do you eat on the couch, or do you wanna sit at the table?"

They'd eaten the spaghetti at Jace's dining room table, but only because he was worried about slopping sauce down his chest. But this casserole wasn't nearly as messy, and he often ate on the go, standing up in the kitchen, or on the couch while he watched the news—mostly the weather. He wasn't sure of the last time he'd actually sat at the table to eat.

"Well, I don't want to miss a minute of that rousing romance," she said as she set the plates next to the stove and retreated.

He laughed as he pulled out forks and spoons. He used a spoon to dollop whipped cream on two pudding cups, sliding one toward her and dipping deep into his cup. He extracted a bite of cake and pudding stained with purple blueberries and stuck it in his mouth.

Immediate regret flooded him. Canned blueberries from a muffin mix should *not* be consumed outside of the actual muffin. He choked, the texture of the pudding not quite right either. He managed to swallow, but it wasn't easy, and he didn't want to take another bite.

"That bad, huh?" she asked.

"It's fine." He reached for a glass and grabbed the ice from the freezer. "Just fine." He put ice in two glasses and filled them with water. "No punch today. Water okay?"

"Water is *just fine.*"

He turned toward her at the bite in her tone and found her with one hip leaned against the counter and a wry smile on her face. "What?"

"You don't like the dessert." She didn't seem upset, those sexy eyes gazing at him with a playful light in them.

"I didn't like the dessert," he said, one corner of his mouth kicking up into a half-smile. "Did you taste it?"

She shook her head and glanced at the pudding cup he'd slid down the counter.

"Try it," he said.

"Just because it's not chocolate doesn't mean it's not good."

"Honey, even if that pudding was chocolate, well, I think that would make it worse." He picked up her cup and erased the few feet between them. "It's not the pudding. That tastes fine. Try it." Caleb dug into her pudding cup, past the whipped cream, to make sure he got a bite with cake, pudding, and those nasty blueberries.

Her eyes sparkled like dark diamonds, and the electricity between them felt as strong as lightning. She shook her head, her lips stubbornly closed.

"Come on." He set the pudding cup on the counter and swept his hand around her waist, bringing her nearly flush against him. "You made it and brought it all the way over here."

"I don't eat dessert before dinner. Didn't your mother teach you that?" The smile she wore as she gazed at him settled all the way into Caleb's soul, and it felt kind and soft.

"I always eat dessert before dinner," he said.

"You've always been somewhat of a rebel."

He inched the spoonful of dessert closer. "Come on. One tiny taste." He dropped his gaze to her lips, his own desire to have one tiny taste skyrocketing. He wondered if he could, right here, right now.

The way Holly gazed up at him, maybe he could. She switched her attention to the spoon and said, "All right." She opened her mouth and waited. Caleb watched her for another moment, her absolute beauty almost overwhelming. A smile snuck across his face, and he stuck the spoon in her mouth.

She closed her lips over it, and he pulled back. He moved back a half-step, but didn't remove his hand from her hip. Her face scrunched up, and he laughed.

"There's something not right here," she said after she swallowed. "I can't believe I got that down. Blech."

He encircled her in his arms and brought her closer. "I kinda want to taste it again," he whispered as she pressed her cheek to his collarbone.

"How is that possible?" Her tone matched his: soft and husky and filed with heat.

"Because I want to kiss you so badly right now." He leaned back and looked down at her, searching for her permission. He smiled and lifted one eyebrow.

She grinned, tipped up on her toes, and paused with just an inch between his mouth and hers. With his heart pounding, he captured her mouth, finally getting the kiss he'd been dreaming of—and it was everything he'd hoped for, vanilla pudding and all.

---

Holly pressed herself against Caleb, glad he had such a tight hold on her because she felt like all her bones and muscles had turned to mush. Her hands slipped inside his arms and up his chest, the kiss continuing and deepening. She cupped his face in her hands and kissed him with everything she had, everything she wanted to give to him, everything she'd been saving for the right person.

He broke the kiss and said, "Wow," before bringing his lips to hers again.

*Wow* didn't even begin to cover what kissing Caleb felt like. Holly had never been kissed like this before, not even by Nathan. There were definite differences between the two brothers, and Holly knew who she preferred.

She giggled and ducked her chin to her chest as he tucked her against his body. "I'm *really* hungry now," he said.

"Worked up an appetite, huh?"

"It takes a lot of energy to keep my hands to myself." He released her and moved back to the stove. Caleb collected a serving spoon from a crock on the counter and dished up the food. "Let's eat."

He handed her a plate and a fork, then picked up his own. "I usually eat on the couch, but we might have to start that movie over. I haven't seen a minute of it."

"Not even the beginning?" They'd watched probably twenty minutes of it before the timer had gone off.

"I can't focus on a movie and try not to kiss you at the same time." He grinned at her, leaned over, and kissed her again. "I'm just a simple cowboy." Something lingered beneath the words, but he turned and went into the living room before Holly had time to examine his face, read his feelings, ask him what that meant.

She left her pudding cup on the counter and followed him, sitting cross-legged on the couch next to him while he restarted the movie. He caught her looking at him, smiled, and picked up his fork. "If you don't like this," he said after his first bite. "I don't know if I'll ever understand you."

She smiled, scooped together a piece of ham and a crispy, breadcrumby piece of chicken and put it in her mouth. The moan that emanated from her chest couldn't be helped, and she couldn't have stopped it even if she wanted to. Her eyes drifted closed, and she said, "That's amazing."

When she opened her eyes and looked at Caleb, he stared at her with a dangerous glint in his eyes. He'd frozen, his fork halfway between his plate and his mouth. "What?"

The spell holding him hostage seemed to break and he shook himself. "Nothing," he mumbled as he stuck his food in his mouth, but a ruddy blush crept up from under his collar. Holly looked down at her food, a distinct warmth radiating from her core. She should've been wondering what she was doing, going to church with Caleb, eating with Caleb, kissing Caleb, when her life here was temporary —and his was decidedly not.

But she didn't want to worry about that. Not right now. Not with his delicious food in front of her, and his delicious smile beside her, and the delicious taste of him still in her mouth. So she just smiled and took another bite.

———

Weeks passed and thankfully, Caleb didn't have any more Sundays off. Holly didn't go down into the valley for church herself, though she had a nice, new truck and could've made it just fine.

Weeks passed, and Caleb invited her to dinner on the nights he wasn't still working when it was time to eat. She enjoyed his company, and his food, and his wit. She was surprised at how easy he was to talk to, and she told him about her veterinary program, the boarding farm where she used to work, and the graduate program she was hoping to apply to in the fall. He'd been reflective after that, and she understood why. It was no secret she wasn't going to be in Gold Valley forever. Not even until the end of the year.

Weeks passed, and he kissed her any time they were alone together. In the barn, against his front door, on the couch, in his kitchen, once right out in the open when she'd gone up to the upper pastures to check on some cattle they'd reintroduced to the main herd.

As she woke, that kiss lingered in her mind the way it always did. That kiss had held such emotion, such kindness, such tenderness. As she brought her fingers to her lips to feel the ghost of that kiss again, she knew she was in real danger of falling in love with Caleb Chamberlain.

The very idea was ridiculous, and yet it lingered in her mind. She'd have to take their relationship out from behind closed doors soon enough, and Holly pushed herself into a seated position, another pressing thought in her mind on this Sabbath day.

She needed to go to church.

Today. She needed to go to church today.

As she thought of the people she'd have to face there—

her parents, Caleb's parents, her old friends, the pastor—her mouth turned dry and her insides shriveled away from the idea. She could wait one more week. Couldn't she?

She got up and went into the bathroom, a war raging in her mind. She'd learned growing up not to ignore feelings and promptings, and she'd felt like she should go to church today. But she hadn't been in so long, and that last time with Caleb had been an utter disaster. She hadn't felt anything during the sermon, and she'd worried for weeks that her faith would always be this dark, this cold, this dead.

She showered, still at odds with herself. She made coffee, and ate a piece of peanut butter toast—something Caleb had introduced her to. Of all his weird food combinations, she had enjoyed the peanut butter toast. She put on a dress and heels, and before she knew it, she'd started her truck so it could warm up before she began the thirty-minute drive down the canyon.

As she settled herself behind the wheel, she took a deep breath and did something she hadn't truly done in a long, long time. She bent her head and closed her eyes and prayed. Really poured her heart and soul into the words, simple and short as they were.

"Please let me feel something at church today." She waited for more to come into her mind, but when nothing did, she planted her hands on the steering wheel and hitched her determination in place.

She was going to church.

When she arrived, the chapel was half-full of chattering people, most of them already sitting in the pews. She glanced around for her parents, thinking she could easily slide onto their bench with them. They didn't seem to be there yet, though, so Holly summoned her bravery and walked down the aisle to the first row that didn't have anyone sitting in it. She moved all the way to the middle and sat down, her fists clenched inside her coat pockets.

Her phone went off, and she hastened to silence it. No one seemed to notice, as the service hadn't started yet, but she silenced it before checking Caleb's text. *You left? Where are you?*

*Church,* she thumbed out.

She could hear his surprise through his text that said, *You went to church alone?*

*Yes,* she sent back. *Now stop texting me. The service is about to start.*

*I would've gone with you.*

*You're working today.*

*Already done with the chores.*

*Come down then.*

*By the time I shower and drive there, it'll be over.*

*Make me lunch then.*

*Deal.*

Holly smiled at her phone, then shoved it in her pocket when the organ began. She'd prayed to feel something today, and in order to do that, she'd need her full attention on the pastor—despite the pull to text Caleb for the next hour.

A family had taken the bench to her left, and a couple sat down on the end of the row to her right. Even if her parents had arrived, they wouldn't climb over people to sit by her. They probably hadn't even looked for her.

So she stood with the congregation for the opening hymn and shrugged out of her coat before she sat down to listen to Dr. Pinnion.

"Brothers and sisters," he began, his voice as warm as hot apple cider on Christmas Eve and his smile sending light to the farthest row in the chapel. "Go and sin no more." He let his words sink in as he scanned the audience from left to right. "That's what the Savior taught, and any who feel like they haven't been forgiven, haven't been able to move forward from something in their past, I want to remind you to go and sin no more. You are forgiven."

Pins and needles pricked the back of Holly's neck, a feeling she hadn't experienced for years. She felt warm and cold at the same time, and a sob worked its way up from her stomach. She managed to swallow it down before it came out.

As Dr. Pinnion continued to talk about how people can change, and that Lord expects people to change, and how others can accept the changes in people, Holly felt something—a love so deep and so enduring, she couldn't fathom it.

She let her tears slide silently down her face, thanking the Lord for His love, and for answering her prayer.

# CHAPTER 12

Holly parked in Caleb's driveway after church, her need to see him almost to the breaking point. She didn't care that her makeup was likely smudged, didn't care that she'd cried on her mother's shoulder in public, didn't care that his parents had given her the cold shoulder again. She just wanted to see him, talk to him, share everything she'd felt and experienced with him.

She knocked on his door and waited, her heart about to burst. He opened the door with his phone to his ear. He didn't smile when he saw her, which took her mood down a notch. He gestured her inside though the weather had started to warm, and said, "I know that, Nathan."

Holly stared at him as she crossed the threshold of his house, all her earlier emotion bleeding away and being replaced with fear and dread.

"So what did you tell Mom and Dad? That's all I need to know." Caleb kept his attention on her as he listened, his eyes storming with frustration. "That can't be true. You should see the way they treat Holly." He listened again for one, two, three breaths before he said, "Look, she's here. I need to go." He hung up without waiting for his brother to say another word and he watched her from his position near the front door. "Hey, there." He exhaled as he set his phone on the table next to the door and moved toward her. He gathered her into the safety of his arms and pressed a kiss to the top of her head.

"You called Nathan?"

"Katie called and said my parents were all up in a tizzy because they saw you at church again today, and how dare you?" He pulled back and smiled at her. "You said hello to them." He ducked his head to kiss her, and she lost herself to Caleb's gentle touch. Something inside her felt more urgent, and she took his tender kiss and turned it into something more intense, something far more dangerous, something more wild.

"Okay," he whispered, pulling back. "What's goin' on?"

"Nothing."

"Holly."

She relented, unable to defend herself against him when he used such a warm tone. "I woke up this morning, thinking about that kiss up in the fields." She stepped out of his arms and slipped her arms out of her coat.

"The kiss up in the fields?" He took her coat and hung it on the hook by the door.

"Yeah." She sighed as she sank onto the couch.

He joined her, sweeping one muscled arm around her shoulders. "So you liked that kiss."

"Don't be so proud of yourself." She gave him a playful jab in the ribs.

He leaned his mouth close to her ear and whispered, "I think about that kiss all the time too."

"Anyway," she said loudly to get him back on the right topic. "I was thinking about us, and I started thinking about my parents, and then your parents, and I suddenly had a feeling I should go to church."

"Hmm." He ran his lips along the side of her face, from her temple to her cheek.

"It was a great sermon. Just what I needed. It wasn't so hard to be there."

"That's great." Caleb straightened and trailed his fingers along her upper arm.

"And yes, I tried to say hello to your parents, but they just looked at me and kept walking. I met the pastor, and he seems nice. I talked to my parents for a few minutes." She continued to tell him how she'd felt, and what had happened at church that morning. He listened, and he asked follow-up questions, encouraging her to ask, "So I'm wondering if next week you want to come with me, and if you'd like to go eat lunch at my parents' house afterward."

Caleb blinked at her, his dreamy eyes wide as he studied her. "What kind of opinions do they have about me?"

"They don't have an opinion about you."

"I'm sure that's not true. They were six months away

from your wedding with *my* brother. Surely they have some opinion of the Chamberlains."

Holly's chest felt like someone had punctured it with an ice pick. "They have an opinion of Nathan. Not you."

The concern in his eyes softened and he looked away. "All right. I'll talk to Jace and see if I can do the early chores again or get the whole day off."

Relief bloomed through Holly. "Great." She glanced into the kitchen, ready for something easy and less serious. "So what did you make for lunch?"

"Always with the food," he grumbled as he stood. "I'm starting to feel used for my culinary skills."

She laughed as she followed him into the kitchen. "You're just starting to feel that way?"

He pulled a pot out of the fridge and practically threw it on a burner. He wrenched the knob to light the flame and turned to glare at her. "Very funny."

"Come on," she said, easing into his personal space and sliding her hands up his chest. "You know I'm not just interested in what you'll be feeding me."

"Do I?"

She looked right into his eyes, right into his soul. He possessed an edge of agony she didn't quite understand. "Caleb." She stretched up and kissed him. He let her, but only for a moment.

"I've never done anything to make you think I'm not interested in you," she said, falling back a few paces and watching him. He wore his cowboy hat, a device he used to conceal his eyes. "What's going on?"

He lifted his eyes to hers. "You sure you want to be with a cowboy?" He gestured around the kitchen. "This is my whole life. This ranch. This life. This is it."

Confusion threaded through her. "I know who you are, Caleb."

"It's a relentless job," he continued. "I won't have every Sunday off. I'll never be foreman. I don't even *want* more than what I have."

"So?" she challenged. This was not the less serious conversation she'd been hoping for. She stared at him, unsure of where this was coming from. "Talk to me, Caleb."

Indecision raced across his face, and she retreated farther from him, taking a seat at the dining room table while he collected a spoon from the dish drainer and turned to stir the soup. The silence seemed to stretch into long strands that lasted far too long, but Holly had a feeling she should wait until he was ready to talk. So she folded her arms, determined to win this waiting game.

———

Caleb stirred and stirred and stirred, his thoughts swirling with the cabbage patch stew he'd thrown together after Holly's text earlier. He wasn't sure why his old insecurities had presented themselves now, and he didn't know what to do with them. But Holly had done something hard, and he thought maybe he could too.

He put the spoon in the sink and faced her. "My ex-girlfriend was not satisfied that I was going to be a cowboy my whole life."

"Robin," she said.

"Robin," he confirmed. He'd mentioned her several times over the past few weeks, but this felt heavier than any of those more casual conversations.

Holly waited, her eyebrows reaching toward her hairline, and Caleb realized in that moment that she was not Robin.

*Of course she's not*, he chastised himself, but for some reason, he'd assumed that all women—including Holly— would want more than what Horseshoe Home Ranch had to offer. Than what *Caleb* had to offer.

"You're leaving in six and a half months," he blurted.

Holly remained seated at the table, her eyes blazing at him from across the kitchen. "This isn't about me, Caleb."

"*I'm* not leaving in six and a half months." He took a deep breath in preparation to say what he hoped wouldn't be the death knell for this relationship. "I'm not leaving the ranch ever."

"I'm not asking you to."

Even the bubbling stew couldn't distract him. "What are we doing here then? I'm not the sharpest tool in the shed, but I can use a computer. I looked up how long a Ph.D in veterinary medicine takes, Holly. Two years. It takes a *minimum* of two years."

She stared back at him evenly. "And?"

"And what?"

"There's more."

There was. There was a lot more, including that he was a selfish man who didn't want to leave the ranch he loved. Including his insecurities and disbelief that a woman could ever be truly with him, a simple cowboy.

"This is enough for now." His words barely registered in his own ears and he turned back to the stove. A few quick stirs and the soup was done. He moved it to a hot pad on the counter and got down two bowls. He pulled a loaf of sour dough from the drawer and stuck four pieces in the toaster.

The silence surrounding him felt suffocating—until Holly sidled up next to him and said, "This looks delicious. Thank you, Caleb." She tilted her head to look at him and he looked down at her. "Everything doesn't have to be decided right now. Anything can happen in six and a half months."

A lot had happened in six and a half weeks, and the tension in Caleb's shoulders eased up a little. Still, he said, "This only ends in one of two ways, Holly, and both of them terrify me."

A ghost of a smile flashed across her face. "Me too, Caleb. Me too."

He drew her into a hug, relieved when she clung to him as tightly as he held her. "Just so I'm clear, I hear you saying you want me to keep cooking for you and keep kissing you, and we'll deal with you leaving for school when it's time for you to leave for school."

She nodded, her chin bobbing against his shoulder. "Yeah, that sounds good."

He drew back. "In the meantime, I'm going to meet your parents as your boyfriend and we're going to figure things out with my parents? Yeah?"

Fear paraded across her face, but she said, "Yeah." She picked up her soup right when the toast popped up. "And I want to know what Nathan told your parents."

Caleb buttered the toast, a sigh starting way down in his toes. "He claims he just told them you were too possessive, and he couldn't deal with that kind of craziness."

"That's obviously not true."

"I know." Caleb handed her two pieces of toast and dunked a spoon in her soup bowl. With his meal in his hands, he started for the couch. "I'll see what else I can find out. Right now, I'm tired and hungry."

"You and me both."

"So we can eat and then take a nap?"

She flashed him a sexy smile. "Sure thing, cowboy."

He grinned, dunked his toast in his stew, and took a buttery, tomato-y bite. "Mm."

"Oh, come on," she said as she watched him with horror on her face. "Do you have to mix everything?"

"Dipping toast in soup is totally normal," he said. "Give it a try." He watched her as she dubiously touched a tiny corner of her toast into her stew and nibbled it.

She lifted one shoulder and dunked the toast in the tomato broth. "All right. This one you're right on. But I am not trying potato chips on a peanut butter sandwich, or potato chips in tomato soup, or potato chips in salsa. Gross."

He grinned and took a bite of his stew as she dipped her toast again. "Okay, sunshine. You eat your potato chips all boring and plain."

"I will." She lifted her chin and sniffed, which elicited a laugh from deep within his chest.

# CHAPTER 13

$\mathcal{C}$aleb slopped through the mud the following Sunday, the sun rising earlier each day as spring started to show itself on the ranch. If there was a season Caleb disliked more than winter, it was spring. He hated having wet feet all the time, and dirt and other undesirables caked up to his knees, and branding season.

He never thought he'd be thankful for the early-morning chores on the weekend, but the ground was only starting to thaw as he finished the morning feeding. He passed Ty and Will on his way back to his cabin and he lifted his hand in a wave. "Mornin'."

"You done already?" Ty called.

"Been out since five," Caleb responded. "Everyone got fed down here, so you're welcome!"

Ty and Will chuckled, and Caleb grinned at them until they went in the horse stables. They'd clean out the stalls and go up to the upper pastures to make sure the fences were intact and the rest of the herd got fed. Caleb threw his jeans straight into the washing machine and stepped into the shower. He'd barely gotten dressed when his phone sounded, indicating that Holly was ready to leave.

He hadn't eaten, hadn't combed his hair, hadn't brushed his teeth. All of those were ultra-important to him today, a day when he wanted to kiss Holly and then meet her parents. He squirted toothpaste on his brush and started brushing as he hurried into the kitchen to make himself a quick bologna sandwich. He spread butter on one piece of bread and mayo on the other, wondering why he was brushing his teeth before eating this concoction.

He spit and rinsed in the kitchen sink before adding pickles, cheddar cheese, and bologna to the bread. Back in the bathroom, he got his hair to cooperate, and he pulled his jacket and hat from the hook as Holly honked again.

He ran down his front steps, his jacket and cowboy hat in one hand and his sandwich in the other. Though the sun shone, his wet hair cracked as it froze. He slid into her passenger seat, noting how much nicer her truck was than his. He whistled as he sat on the leather. "Nice outfit."

She glanced down at her black skirt covered with little ruffles. "Thanks." She laughed and backed onto the ranch road.

"Can't wait to see what's under the coat." He balanced his sandwich on the dashboard and put on his jacket and hat before fastening his seat belt. He'd just bit into his breakfast when she gasped. "What?"

"What are you eating?"

"Bologna sandwich." He tilted it toward her and took another bite.

"With pickles?"

He ignored her incessant food questions. "So can I see what's under the coat?"

"You have such a one-track mind."

"I like your clothes," he said. "And frankly, I'm hurt you didn't say how nice my shirt is."

"I like your shirt," she deadpanned.

"Can I see yours?"

She sighed but wore a smile as she unbuttoned the first few buttons on her coat. A bright pink top peeked out from behind the black coat. It contrasted well with her dark skin, hair, and eyes. He whistled again.

She rolled her eyes and switched on the radio. The closer they got to church, the more nervous Caleb got. He wasn't sure why. He'd met a woman's parents before, and though he hadn't interacted with Holly's mom and dad recently, he certainly knew who they were.

"Did you tell your mom and dad about me?"

"Sort of," she said. "I told them I was bringing a friend over for lunch after church."

Caleb's heart shrank to the size of a dime. "A friend?"

"My boyfriend."

"Oh, I bet your mom asked a million questions."

"Only about a thousand." She cut him a wry look out of the corner of her eye. "We're sitting by ourselves, right?"

"Right." He hadn't even told Katie he was coming to

church today. "In the back or on the left side." His parents always sat in the middle section, on the right.

She pulled into the parking lot and cut the engine, but they both just sat there. Caleb launched himself into action. "Come on, sunshine. Don't want to be late." He got out of the truck and hurried around the front to be near her when she got out. He took her hand in his as they walked toward the front door.

He didn't glance around, didn't care who was staring. *Let them stare*, he thought. He liked Holly Gray—a lot—and he was tired of hiding it. He relaxed once they'd escaped from the wind, and gave Holly a quick smile. He started to tell her a joke about the weather when he realized she was staring further into the lobby. "Oh, no."

"What?" Caleb swung his head around, his eyes finding the source of her dread immediately: her parents. Her mother stood about the same height as Holly, with the same dark hair, coffee-colored eyes, and slight build. Her father towered next to the petite woman, with white hair shaved close to his scalp and blue eyes. Caleb couldn't see any of the man in Holly, who looked like a younger image of her Hispanic mother.

"I guess you're meeting them now." Holly linked her hand through Caleb's elbow and kept him close to her side.

"Guess you shoulda gone with bringing a *friend* for dinner," he muttered as they started across the lobby. She giggled quietly, cutting off the sound before her parents could hear.

"Hey, Mom." Holly stepped out of Caleb's reach and gave

her mom a hug. "Daddy." She spun and stood next to them, three pairs of eyes now focused on Caleb. "This is my boyfriend—"

"Nathan?" her dad asked. Caleb's muscles turned to ice, and he didn't quite know how to do more than the involuntary bodily functions of breathing and blinking.

"Darrel," her mom admonished. "Of course this isn't Nathan." She wore a smile and took one step before leaning up to kiss Caleb's cheek. "This is *Caleb* Chamberlain."

"Ma'am." Caleb swept his cowboy hat off his head, pure appreciation flowing through him. Her mother had *seen* him, really seen him. "Sir." He extended his hand and Darrel shook it, a pinch around his eyes that didn't disappear with his smile. At least he hadn't reacted the way Caleb's parents had.

"I'm looking forward to lunch," Caleb said, claiming Holly's hand for solidarity and strength. "It'll be a nice change from me laboring in the kitchen every evening. Your daughter is a real slave driver."

"I am not." She playfully slapped his bicep. "I don't make him cook for me every night."

Her mom and dad stood there, smiling a bit woodenly in Caleb's opinion. He stepped toward the chapel in the hopes of ending this conversation as quickly as possible. "She really does," he added with a chuckle. He steered her toward a bench in the back, on the left, as they'd planned. He didn't want to be rude, so he said, "You wanna sit with us?"

Holly's mother exchanged a glance with Holly, who must've been able to communicate telepathically, because she said, "No, we like to sit a little closer." They continued down the aisle, much to Caleb's relief.

He sat, leaving only enough room for Holly to squeeze in next to him, and put his arm around her. He leaned down and kissed her temple. "That was close."

"They're just glad I'm dating again," she whispered, nestling an inch closer to him.

"So am I," he said. When she tilted her face back to look at him, he bent down and kissed her—right there in the chapel. Holly tensed in his arms but kissed him back.

---

Holly had whispered, "Behave yourself," to Caleb after that kiss, and thankfully, he had. Dr. Pinnion delivered another sermon that spoke to Holly's soul. A sermon about trusting in the path God had chosen. As she listened, she wondered if all the twists, all the heartache, all the disappointments had led her to Caleb specifically. Led her to Gold Valley at this particular time.

Dr. Pinnion said they did, and that the Lord knew what He was doing, even when things didn't work out the way she wanted them to. And Holly felt the truth in his words, and she left church for the second week in a row with a new perspective on her life.

Afterward, Holly hoped to make a quick escape, but she hadn't last week when she'd come by herself, and there was no way her circling girlfriends were letting her get away without explaining the handsome man she hung on.

Angie was the first to pounce, waiting as she was right outside the chapel doors. "Holly." She gave Holly a quick side hug. "Good to see you here again." Her gaze switched to Caleb. "Hello, Caleb."

Caleb stuck his hat back on his head and said, "Ma'am."

Angie giggled, and Holly introduced them.

"I know who she is," Caleb said. "I know them all." He waved at the three other loitering women to come on over. "This is Bonnie, Jasper Paulson's wife, and…." He leaned closer to Holly and put up one hand to speak behind. "Word on the street is that she's got a little love affair with *cheese.*" He said the last word like it was something horrible.

Holly blinked at him once before tipping her chin back and filling the whole lobby with laughter. The other women joined in, something that set Holly at ease.

"Should I go on?" Caleb asked, his hands stuck in his front pockets as he rocked back on his heels, obviously pleased with himself.

"Oh, I think we've got it." Holly laced her fingers through his and beamed up at him. He looked down at her with the sweetest look of adoration, something she hadn't seen on a man's face in years. "Well, we're going to lunch with my parents, so we better head out."

The women parted, letting Holly and Caleb move through. He spoke to the pastor, but Holly hovered a half-step behind him, unwilling to say much this week. Last week, she'd wiped her eyes as she pumped his hand with both of hers and said he'd given a beautiful sermon. He caught her eye with a smile and a nod and let her go.

Though she hadn't been tense, now that church was over and she'd fared much better than last time she'd shown up with Caleb, an invisible band of tension binding her lungs evaporated. She released a breath she hadn't realized had been trapped.

"So we're headed over there right now?" Caleb asked as he glanced at her.

"Yep." She unlocked the truck and climbed in, taking a few seconds to adjust her skirt while he leaned in her door. "That wasn't too bad, was it?"

"Not too bad at all, sunshine." He kissed her, and though it wasn't with the careful passion and absolute desire of their first kiss, it felt like it all over again. Caleb had been very gentlemanly in his affections, never pressuring her to move faster than she wanted to, or kiss longer than was appropriate. He kicked her out of his cabin every evening by nine o'clock, claiming that five came really early for a cowboy at Horseshoe Home Ranch who didn't get his sleep.

She threaded her fingers through his hair and kissed him again after he pulled back. When the kiss ended, she simply looked at him and he looked back at her. The depth of emotion she felt dictated that she might be nearly in love with him, but she didn't want to say it first. The way his eyes swam with love and desire, she thought she could wait for him to vocalize things between them.

"Get in, cowboy," she finally whispered. "It's freezing out there." She slid over on the seat and extended the keys toward him.

"You want me to drive?"

"Sure. You remember where my parents live?"

He climbed into the truck, but she hadn't left him enough room, so she scooted over a smidge more. "I, uh, maybe have been one of their regular garden thieves and I moved you out of their basement a couple of months ago. So yeah, I know where they live."

She giggled and leaned her head against his arm as he started the truck. "Better not tell my father about the vegetable pilfering."

"Pretty sure he already knows," Caleb said. "That's why he was all glarey in the lobby."

"Come on. Who holds a grudge for a decade?"

"Well, my parents have been for half that." The mood sobered after that, and Holly searched through her thoughts and memories to find something that would make Caleb's parents dislike her so much.

"Nathan must have told them *some*thing," she said.

"I asked Katie, and she said he really didn't. He just said you were really jealous, and ultra clingy, and you didn't trust him and he couldn't be with someone like that."

Holly suddenly wished she'd driven, because Caleb would've never slid across the seat and ridden right next to her. She felt like she needed more space to think, more oxygen to breathe, until she could figure things out.

"Do you think I'm really jealous and clingy and distrusting?"

"No," he said. "I've never seen you act like that."

"But?" she prompted, because there was a definite "but" on the end of his statement.

"But nothing." He cut her a glance out of the corner of his eye.

She reminded herself that *right this second* she was acting distrusting, not believing what he said. Not what she thought he'd said. Not what she'd interpreted his words to mean. But what he'd actually said.

"There's a reason I acted crazy with him," she said.

Caleb's knuckles tightened on the steering wheel. Holly continued, "Do you know his wife, Mel?"

"Yeah, I mean, a little. He's been gone to dental school for three years, and they only got married the year before that. I had just gotten in my car accident…so I don't know her that well."

"She was the one I thought Nathan was meeting, you know, when he said he was studying. I saw him and Mel together. They texted all the time. I thought he was cheating on me."

Caleb sucked in a breath and looked at her longer than was safe for someone who was driving. "Really?" He glanced back to the road.

"They were in three classes together," Holly said, following his gaze. "They met every night of the week. Their class would get out early, but he'd get home at normal time, because he was with her. When I asked him about Mel, he denied everything. Called me crazy and paranoid and…." Her voice drifted into silence and she shook the cobwebs of his poisoned words from her mind. "And then he married her less than a year after we broke up. It sort of cemented all my suspicions that they were more than friends while we were engaged."

The radio she'd turned on earlier warbled a country song about exes, and Holly found it profoundly fitting. The silence between her and Caleb felt different, but not difficult, and she found herself lost in her own thoughts.

If she had changed, maybe Nathan had too. That thought blasted through her mind like a speeding bullet. She'd gotten over Nathan; she had. She wasn't in love with him and harbored no hope that she would be again.

But maybe she hadn't forgiven him quite yet.

"Do you think people can change?" she asked.

"I'm living proof that people change," Caleb said. "What is goin' on inside your head? Just nervous about me coming to lunch?"

"No." She sighed and fought to order her words. "I'm just…I've changed a lot since my relationship with Nathan."

"I believe it."

"But no one else seems to notice."

"Why do you care if they notice?"

"Because…." she started, but she didn't know how to finish, so she said, "I don't know."

"Look." Caleb enveloped her hand in his. "All that matters is what you know, and what the Lord knows. And what you choose to do based on the kind of person you want to be." He pulled up to the red light and turned toward her. "And you're a kind, caring, compassionate woman." He kissed her, quick and chaste. "And real pretty too." He punctuated his statement with a smile and pressed on the gas when the light turned green.

A few minutes later, he pulled up to the curb in front of her parents' home. "All right. Lips sealed about the stealing of fall squashes and I believe you said I couldn't kiss you in front of them. So maybe we should do that before we go in." He grinned at her, his face devilishly handsome, his hands warm and strong as they moved around her waist and drew her against him.

As she kissed Caleb Chamberlain, all thoughts and cares about his brother vanished. She simply gave up her attachment to Nathan, and finally forgave him for his treatment of her all those years ago.

# CHAPTER 14

*J*f Holly had known how freeing forgiving could be, she'd have done it long ago. Of course, that would've required her to go to church, and she hadn't been in a good mental or emotional state for that.

She stopped mid-step on her parents' sidewalk. "God really does lead us on this topsy-twisty road to get us where we need to be."

Caleb chuckled. "I believe He does, sunshine. Can we talk about it inside?" He tugged on her hand and they hurried up to the front door, where Holly knocked and entered without waiting. This time, Caleb froze, and she turned back, a question in her eyes.

"Do you really think they'll come around to liking me?"

Holly didn't mind his brief moment of insecurity. It was actually nice to know the man experienced such things. "Of course." She gestured for him to follow her. "It would be impossible for them not to like you."

———

The smell of roasted meat and gravy was all the convincing Caleb needed to enter the house. If Holly's mother could cook like this, why couldn't Holly? After the disappointing blueberry shortcakes, she hadn't even attempted another dish—dessert or otherwise. He kept giving her tips on different kinds of sandwiches she could try, but she was dead set against putting chili-cheese corn chips between bread. He didn't understand it.

There was one flavor combination he'd hooked her on though—vanilla bean ice cream with a pretzel as a spoon. Even better if he could get down to the valley—or get Jace's approval—for the chocolate caramel covered pretzels. In fact, he thought he might stop by the grocery store before they headed back up the canyon this afternoon. Then he could enjoy the sweet treat with his girlfriend.

"Something smells amazing," he said as Georgia appeared, wearing an apron and wiping her hands on a dishtowel. He grinned at her, and her smile seemed genuine enough. It was Darrel Gray that needed the convincing, and Caleb glanced around for Holly's dad.

"Daddy's not feeling well," Georgia said, her face falling for half a heartbeat. "But the roast is ready. Do you like cooked carrots, Caleb?"

"I like anything, ma'am."

Holly snorted as she entered the kitchen. "He's not lying, Mom. I've seen him eat some of the most disgusting things."

"Not true," Caleb countered.

Georgia watched Holly for a moment and then Caleb before she lifted the plate with steaming meat, potatoes, carrots, and onions and set it in the middle of the dining room table. "Grab that gravy, would you, Caleb? And Holly, get the basket of rolls."

The conversation with Holly's mom was easy, but Caleb didn't believe for a moment that her husband was ill. He just didn't want to spend any time with Caleb. Fully satiated, Caleb leaned back and employed his boldest side. "So, Georgia, what's the real reason Darrel didn't want to eat lunch with me?"

Holly gasped, her eyes wide and frantic as she first looked at Caleb and then her mother.

"No reason."

"Ma'am." Caleb spoke quietly, the way he would to a spooked horse. "If it walks like a duck, and quacks like a duck, it's probably a duck."

Holly's foot found his under the table, but he ignored her and moved his boots back so she couldn't kick him again.

"It has nothing to do with you," Georgia said.

Caleb chuckled, the sound dark and dangerous even to his own ears. "I think it does, ma'am. I'm the one who's here and he won't even come out and say hello." He glanced at Holly, looking for backup. "Holly?"

She set her eyes on that fiery Latina that got Caleb's blood pumping a little hotter and a lot faster. "Mom?"

Georgia threw her napkin down on her empty plate. "It's just that—" She cut a glance to Caleb. "When your brother broke Holly's heart, that killed Darrel. She's our only daughter, and well, I'm afraid he lost his temper."

Holly seemed as riveted to the story as Caleb was. "Go on," he said cautiously, finally getting to something he could chew on, figure out.

"He went over to your house to talk to your father. It did not go well. We haven't spoken to your parents in five years." She crossed her arms and clamped her lips shut.

Caleb stared at her, his mind playing catch-up. Holly's hand landed on his arm, her fingernails digging into his skin. "That's why they don't like me, Caleb," she said. "It has nothing to do with what Nathan told them. It was my father."

"And mine," Caleb said darkly. "Georgia, when you say it didn't go well, what does that mean?"

She stood and picked up her plate and glass. "I have no issue with you, Caleb. I think you're a nice man. Hardworking and handsome…." She met Holly's eyes. "It's clear my daughter thinks you're made of gold. I wasn't there when Darrel went over to your house. I begged him not to go. But I was here when he came home bleeding. I made him go to the emergency room and everything." She marched into the kitchen and put her plate in the sink, the clatter of dishware against stainless steel jolting through Caleb the same way her words had.

She left them sitting at the dining room table, and Caleb slowly brought his eyes to Holly's. "My father hit yours?" He sat back, stunned. "I have no idea—I can't imagine him doing that."

Holly shook her head, her eyes as wide and filled with disbelief as Caleb felt coursing through him. "Me either."

Several minutes passed while Caleb tried to make sense of everything.

"What do we do now, Caleb?" Holly asked.

He inhaled, feeling the way his muscles bunched and stretched. "We go get some pretzels to eat with our ice cream." He stood and reached for her hand. "Come on, sunshine. Let's go put on a movie, eat some ice cream, and take a nap."

She placed her hand in his with a smile and a shake of her head. "Always food for you," she said. "We just ate!"

"Wait until I show you what kind of pretzels I'm going to buy."

# CHAPTER 15

Caleb finished off the last chocolate-covered caramel pretzel and peered into the ice cream container. "Still some left. Want me to scoop it and put maple syrup on it?"

"Maple syrup on ice cream?" Holly barely glanced at him, and her voice had lost its level of incredulity over his "strange" food combinations.

"It's delicious." He started to get up, and she put her hand on his chest. "I'm stuffed, so don't dish me any."

He put the ice cream back in the freezer and returned to the living room. "It's getting late, sunshine." He stifled a yawn.

She groaned as she stood. "Yeah, and five o'clock comes early." She smiled and stepped into him, her fingers tiptoeing up his chest. "Isn't that what you always say?"

He received her gladly into his embrace, trailing his lips along her neck to her ear. "If you got up at five, you'd understand." He nuzzled her neck before moving to her mouth for a goodnight kiss. The sweet treat had helped to take his mind off his parents, but nothing could quite make him forget about everyone and everything the way kissing Holly could.

He pulled back right when he wanted to accelerate. "See you tomorrow." He leaned against the kitchen table and watched her from under the brim of his hat. He found the flush in her face beyond attractive, the way she tucked her hair behind her ear adorable, the fact that she couldn't stop smiling satisfying.

She put on her coat and turned back to him from the front door. "I'm meeting with Jace in the morning, so I probably won't see you until lunchtime."

"Sounds good." Caleb told himself he'd let her walk out. He'd already kissed her goodnight. But there was something about her that lit him all the way up.

She started to open the door and he said, "Just a second." He crossed the room in the time it took her to turn back, and he swept in to kiss her again. He wasn't sure why he tried to resist kissing her at the front door. Maybe to prove to himself that he could—too bad he'd failed every time, thus not proving anything to anyone.

Holly's giggle branded itself onto his heart, and he finally let her go before stumbling into his bedroom and falling into bed. As he stared up in the darkness, a giddy smile stuck to his face, he thanked the Lord for bringing such an amazing woman into his life.

His grin faded when his thoughts switched to his

parents. He needed to talk to them, and the sooner the better. He just needed to get all the facts lined up first—and that started with Katie and Nathan.

He sat up and pulled his phone from his back pocket. Caleb didn't want to get drawn into a long-winded explanation, so he simply sent them both the same text: *Do you know anything about our parents and Holly's parents not getting along?*

After he changed into his pajamas, after he brushed his teeth, after he made sure everything was cleaned up and locked down, he checked his phone again. Neither of them had answered.

Caleb frowned, the stream of unease winding through him morphed into a river. "Nothing to do about it now," he muttered to himself and went to bed. His dreams featured Holly—they had for weeks and weeks—but this time the shadows bore the faces of his parents and hers.

––––––––

Holly tossed and turned, Caleb's concerns in her mind. She was scheduled to apply for her graduate program in just a few weeks. She hadn't told Caleb, but that was what her meeting with Jace was about. She needed him to sign off on her intern hours—and she hoped she had enough.

Her original plan had been to complete her internship at Horseshoe Home while she lived with her parents and found a job in the valley. But when he'd called and offered her a bona fide job on the ranch as a veterinary technician—with free room and board—she's snatched up the opportunity. The only problem was, she needed unpaid hours for her program and she might not have enough because of all the work she'd done to get the herd healthy again.

As she turned from right to left for what felt like the twentieth time, she told herself that maybe she just wouldn't apply for her large-animal care graduate program. She didn't need it. She'd ask Jace if she could stay on the ranch with the qualifications she had—and she suspected she could.

Which made her mind churn over why she should leave Gold Valley for a second time, especially when things seemed to be going so well with Caleb. He was obviously worried about her limited time in town, and she could ease that burden from his shoulders.

But the side of her that had sustained her these past five years barked at her not to sacrifice her future because of a man. She finally rolled to her back and opened her eyes. "What should I do?" she said into the darkness. She'd never really stopped praying, but she certainly didn't make it a priority to ask the Lord what He would have her do.

She strained to hear something, anything. She couldn't.

Disappointed and feeling a bit foolish, she turned to her side and closed her eyes. She woke in the morning, no closer to a solution. Her eyes felt like someone had rubbed sand in them, and she arrived in Jace's office a bit sluggish and about five minutes late.

He glanced up from his desk when she said, "Good morning," and sat in the chair across from him. She set the folder containing her school papers on the edge of the desk as he studied her. Caleb had often said Jace could somehow read minds, and as she kept her eyes on his, she felt like she was giving him a clear view into her brain.

"You wanna close the door?" he asked.

Confusion raced through her and her heart tapped a bit harder. "No, it's fine."

Jace put both palms on the desk and pushed himself up with a groan. "I think we should close the door." He walked around the desk and did so, staying behind her until she turned. "I know you want to talk about your internship hours, your job here, and all that. But I want to start with something personal." He crossed his arms and the way he stood with his feet shoulder-width apart made him seem powerful and intimidating.

"All right," she said, keeping her chin toward him.

"I know you're dating Caleb Chamberlain."

"We haven't kept it a secret."

"He told you much about his past?"

"Quite a bit, yeah."

Jace nodded and glanced around his office as if getting approval from an invisible council of cowboys. "He's my Number Two," he finally said. "He means a lot to me. You pickin' up what I'm puttin' down?"

Holly stood too, her blood racing through her veins. Though she stood several inches shorter than Jace—than every cowboy on this blasted ranch—she could hold her own. "I'm not going to hurt him."

Jace chin-nodded toward the folder. "You sure?"

"Can we just talk about what I need you to sign?"

"Sure, of course." He marched back to his place behind his desk, but he didn't sit down. "I know your graduate program means a lot to you."

"It does," she said, questioning herself even as she said the words. "So I need three hundred hours, and I can accomplish that by the end of July, as you can see here." She slid him the top paper in the folder. "I have to turn in my plan for completing the hours if they're not complete by June first. Which these won't be."

Jace barely looked at the paper before signing it. "What else?"

"I appreciate you employing me on the ranch, getting me into a cabin so fast…." She paused, not quite sure how to phrase what she wanted to ask without revealing more to Jace than she was ready to.

"We needed you," he said. "We still do."

"About that." She picked up her folder and hugged it to her chest as the words came to her mind. "What if I don't get into my program? Might I be able to stay on here as Horseshoe Home's veterinary technician?"

"I don't see why not." Jace looked straight into her soul again. "Do you think that's a possibility? You not getting into your program?"

With relief flowing through her and a smile on her face, she said, "Anything's possible, foreman. You should know that."

He chuckled, the first crack that showed he was a real person, and said, "I sure do, Miss Gray." He stood and reached across his desk to shake her hand.

She left his office with the signed paperwork she needed, but her heart still in knots and still in a battle with her brain. With the opportunity to stay right where she was—but maybe move two doors down—she wondered why she needed to go to school for two more years. Pay tuition for two more years. Keep running from herself and everyone she knew for two more years.

So consumed with her thoughts, she collided with a cowboy as she exited the administration lodge and he entered. "Whoa, there."

Holly dropped her folder, her adrenaline shooting into the sky. "Sorry," she said to Ty. He bent to get her papers and handed them back to her. "Thanks."

He flashed his playboy smile, the one she'd seen him wear whenever there was a pretty woman around, which admittedly didn't happen often at the ranch. "I'd avoid Caleb for a while," he said.

Holly scanned the yard beyond the lodge but couldn't see Caleb. Just mud and melting snow and trucks stuck in mud and melting snow. The barns sat behind the administration lodge, and she suspected he'd be back there. "Why?" she asked.

"We were sort of horsing around, and he may or may not have fallen headlong into the mud." Ty's smile was infectious and when he burst into laughter, Holly grinned too. "It was really funny," he said through the chuckles. "Just don't tell him I said that."

"So where is he now?" she asked as Ty started to walk away.

"He went home to change."

She turned back to the ranch, then back to the lodge, an idea forming in her mind. She wasn't on the clock today— all her hours would be intern hours. And she needed them, but she also needed to get a few things clear for her relationship with Caleb to continue.

She hustled back to Jace's office and cleared it with him to go down into the valley. Then, before she could talk herself out of it—or before she could find Caleb and consult with him—she jumped behind the wheel of her truck and went to get her haircut.

# CHAPTER 16

"Come on over." Katie grinned at Holly like not a day had gone by that they hadn't spoken. But the truth was, Holly had abandoned everyone when she'd left Gold Valley. At least it seemed like Nathan hadn't said anything damaging about her, even if he had gotten married so soon after their breakup.

Holly gave Katie a hug. "I just need a little trim."

Katie fingered her hair. "You want some highlights?"

"Do you have time for that?" Holly certainly wasn't the only one waiting at the salon.

"I don't have another appointment until two," she said. "So we could even go to lunch after."

Holly smiled. "Highlights and lunch sound great." She searched for a way to bring up the rift between her parents and Katie's, but nothing felt natural.

"So you're dating my brother...again." Katie snapped a

cape on Holly and laughed, easing the jolt of apprehension that had landed against Holly's heart with her words.

Holly met her friend's eye in the mirror. "Seems that way."

"Come on over to the bowl and we'll wash." Katie led the way, and Holly answered her questions about the ranch, and dating a cowboy, and anything else she asked about Caleb. It was easy conversation, and nothing too personal or gossipy.

It also opened just the door Holly needed. "So do you know why your parents dislike me so much?"

Katie's eyebrows collapsed into a V, but she quickly wiped the frown away. "Caleb asked me the same thing last night. Wanted to know if I knew anything about a problem between your parents and mine."

Impressed with Caleb's behind-the-scenes communication with his siblings, Holly nodded. "Yeah, we went to dinner at my parents' house yesterday after church, and my mom said some things that got us thinking."

"What kind of things?" Katie snipped here and trimmed there, keeping her eyes on her work. Holly didn't see a reason not to tell her, so she did.

Katie froze, much the same way Caleb had. "No." She shook her head. "That can't be true. My dad wouldn't hit someone."

Holly shrugged under the cape. "We're trying to figure it out."

"People aren't perfect," Katie said. "I just can't imagine my father doing that." She got back to work. "Do you think maybe your dad…never mind."

"No, what?" Holly asked.

Katie straightened again and met Holly's eye in the mirror. "I don't want you to be mad."

"Katie, just say it."

"Do you think your dad could've made it up?"

Holly cocked her head to the side and searched Katie's face. "You think he made himself bleed and blamed it on your dad?"

"Of course not." Katie gave a forced laugh. "It sounds stupid when you say it like that."

"All of it is stupid," Holly said. "So Nathan and I didn't work out. Who cares?" An inexplicable anger came with her outburst. "He moved on, I changed. Why does it matter now?"

Katie smoothed Holly's hair. "It doesn't matter now, honey."

Holly scoffed, almost a snort. "My dad wouldn't even come out of his bedroom to eat dinner with me and Caleb."

Katie's snipping stuttered. "Really?"

"And your mom won't even look at me, even when I speak directly to her." She shook her head though she should've kept still for Katie. "Your dad practically yelled to the entire congregation that I wasn't welcome at their house." She sighed, some of her fury getting replaced with frustration. "So something happened, but we don't know what."

"Hmm." Katie cut, cut, cut. "I think it's cute that you keep saying 'we.'"

Holly's insides seized, but she somehow managed to

laugh. Katie spun her toward the window, and their conversation lulled. A familiar truck pulled into the diner's parking lot across the street, and there was no mistaking Caleb's strong gait after he got out of the vehicle.

Her heart stopped as she watched him bend down and lift a cutesy, blonde woman off her feet in a big ole cowboy hug. He set her on her feet and they went into the diner together.

She blinked, sure she hadn't seen what she thought she had. Numbness spread from her brain to the rest of her body, and she couldn't seem to move her fingers or her toes.

*Caleb isn't Nathan,* she started reciting. And reciting. And reciting.

———

Caleb sat across from Missy, a woman he'd danced with a time or two a few summers ago. She was nice, easy on the eyes, but there had been no spark between them. If anything, she was the second little sister he'd never had. And best of all, she was a nurse at the Gold Valley Hospital.

"Your leg looks like it's all healed up nice," she said.

"Pretty good, yeah." He signaled to the waitress that he needed coffee. "How've you been?"

She held out her left hand. "Got married last summer."

He whistled at the rock on her ring finger. "Who's the lucky guy?"

She flashed him a coy smile. "Doctor Bills." She waggled

her finger at him. "I told you four years ago when you were on my rounds that I was gonna marry me a doctor."

Caleb laughed as a cup of steaming coffee was set in front of him. "That you did, Missy." He turned to the waitress and asked if they had any flavored coffee creamers. He'd grown quite fond of them since spending time at Holly's. Though she wasn't talented in cooking, she could make a mean cup of coffee.

"So I know you didn't ask to meet me to shoot the breeze," Missy said after the waitress left.

Caleb sighed, especially when the waitress returned with only regular creamer and hazelnut. While that was Holly's favorite, Caleb preferred chocolate. "No," he said. "I actually wondered if you could find out about someone who's been to the hospital."

He watched her carefully, and sure enough, her lips pursed. "Caleb, I'm not allowed to talk about patients."

"I know, I know." He curled his fingers around his coffee mug. "I don't want you to. I'm just wondering if *I* can get hospital records for a patient if they've ever been in the hospital, or the emergency room...." He let his words hang there, not wanting to get into too many details.

"Well, we have records, sure. But not just anyone can see them. You'd need a warrant or be a family member or a doctor who needs to see them or something like that."

"So a family member could see a hospital record?"

"Potentially."

*Potentially* was good enough for him, and he doused his coffee with the hazelnut creamer and asking for a to-go cup. After all, he didn't have the day off the way Holly did. He just needed to make a little progress on his problems before they drove him insane.

On the drive back to the ranch, he puzzled through how he and Holly could check and see if her father had really gone to the emergency room five years ago. He wasn't sure why his mind had hinged on this piece of information—maybe because both of his texts to his brother and sister had profited him nothing. Neither one of them knew anything about any problems between the two families, though Nathan had said he wouldn't be surprised if there was. He claimed Holly's father had always been overprotective of her, and he could've seen their breakup as something he needed to get involved with to protect Holly.

Caleb wasn't so sure as Holly seemed perfectly capable of taking care of herself. But she could've—no, she *was*—a completely different person than she'd been when she was with Nathan. Caleb knew she'd changed; it was the only thing he clung to when he thought about actually marrying the woman Nathan had also dated.

With such serious thoughts of marriage, Caleb then had to examine his feelings for Holly. He wasn't sure if he loved her, but he knew his life wouldn't be the same without her. He'd thought all he needed was his cabin, his simple life on the ranch, his cowboy buddies, but with her, he realized he actually did want more.

Not just more. He wanted her.

He grinned as he pulled under the double-H arch and bumped across the muddy ruts toward the ranch. His leg jarred against the movement, and he increased his speed to get through the potholes faster. He didn't bother checking in with Jace when he got back. He just went straight to work, having lost about an hour and a half of daylight.

He'd noticed that Holly's truck was gone earlier, but he hadn't texted her. He wanted to have something concrete to discuss with her and he had a little inkling of something now. So he pulled out his phone and texted, *Where'd you go?*

She didn't answer by the time he arrived in the horse barn, so he stuffed his phone in his back pocket and went to exercise his favorite horse, Bullseye.

By the time he returned to his cabin, all the horses had had their exercise time. His boots and the cuffs of his jeans were laden with mud, and he'd had to run the washing machine again, especially after this morning's incident.

He shook he head as he thought of Ty and his antics, a chuckle tickling his vocal chords. One step through his front door, though, and all thoughts of pranks and smiling fled.

"There you are." Holly rose from his couch, a perfect storm of fury. He could scent it on the air, and he wondered what had happened. She'd never answered his text, and he realized now that he'd had a clue to her anger and he'd missed it.

"Hey," he said, stepping all the way inside and closing the door. "What are you doin' here?"

"Waiting for you, obviously." She cocked that hip, but it didn't feel adorable now. She crossed her arms, and Caleb backed into the closed door.

"Your hair looks nice," he tried, his escape blocked by the woman he never wanted to disappoint.

"Really? You're going to resort to flattery?"

Exhaustion swept over Caleb. "Why are you mad?" He walked toward the kitchen, thoughts of dinner on his mind. He hadn't actually eaten at the diner, and he hadn't come in for lunch either.

He'd pulled out a loaf of bread and a package of hot dogs before she said, "I saw you at the diner," in a freaky calm voice that didn't belong to her.

Caleb turned back to her slowly, his ears surely playing tricks on him. "What?"

"The salon is right across the street from the diner. I saw you pull in and give that blonde woman a welcome for the books."

He blinked; his stomach growled; his feet ached. Then he laughed. He laughed at the fire in her eyes. Laughed as he set a pan on the stove and tossed four hot dogs in. Laughed as he smeared his bread with honey to use as a makeshift bun.

"Stop laughing," she said. "It's not funny."

"Oh, it is, sunshine." He abandoned his food prep to face her again. "I met with Missy Bills, wife to Doctor Elliot Bills. She works at the hospital." He spoke slowly, so Holly couldn't misinterpret a single word. "I got a cup of coffee to go—and by the way, the diner would be improved if they had your taste in coffee creamers—and I asked her how we could get our hands on a hospital record."

Holly sputtered, her fire diminishing as a blush erupted in her face. "I—well, I—"

Caleb turned and shook the pan housing his spitting hot dogs, turned down the flame, and walked over to Holly, who stood on the threshold of the kitchen, one foot on the new tile Belle had chosen and one on the carpet Jace had helped pick out during the ranch remodel a few years ago.

Caleb took both of her hands in his, but she was made of cement, unyielding and stiff. "I also texted my sister and my brother. Neither of them knew anything about any problems between our parents and yours."

She gazed up at him, a fearful edge in her eyes. "I'm acting paranoid and crazy, aren't I?"

He smiled softly at her and dipped his mouth to hers for a quick taste. "Yes, sunshine. You are." He kissed her again, this time longer and with more passion. "I like your fiery side, though." He chuckled as he slid his lips to the hollow of her throat. "Very sexy."

Pulling back, she said, "I'm sorry."

"Maybe you can channel some of that Latina flair into making it up to me later," he said. "Right now, I'm starving and I need to start a load of laundry." He gave her a smile with as much energy as he could muster being as hungry, cold, and muddy as he was.

"I'll watch these." She moved over to the stove, her hands hovering above the handle of the pan.

"Just give 'em a shake," he said. "So they don't get charred on one side, okay? I'll go change and get my laundry going."

He left her standing in his kitchen, and he hoped she wouldn't burn the place down by the time he got back.

# CHAPTER 17

$\mathcal{C}$aleb's night got exponentially better after he'd eaten and talked with Holly. And boy, did she know how to make amends for her mistakes. He'd never been kissed like that, and he was sure he would never be again. He didn't even want another woman to kiss him, ever.

As he lay on his couch with Holly tucked against his chest, he stared at the TV but he didn't watch it. He thought maybe he'd fallen in love with Holly Gray. Instead of making him giddy and lightheaded, he felt heavy and worried. If he gave her his whole heart, he feared she'd crack it right in two when she left for her graduate program.

So he held back. He stopped kissing her when he wanted to continue. He held her close but not as close as he could. And when nine o'clock came, he shifted and said it was time for her to go.

He wondered if she could feel the space between them, if she could sense the way he was reserving the best part of himself. If she could, she didn't let on, and he kissed her against his front door with as much passion as he always had and they laughed about her misunderstanding, but the way he plodded to bed and stared out his bedroom window into the darkness was no joke.

———

As spring arrived at the ranch, Caleb gave new meaning to the word busy. Holly kept her head down and tried to keep up with everything happening. From planting, to calving, to branding, she absorbed it all, learned as much as she could, and helped wherever she was needed. Jace consulted with her on the calving, and he assigned her to oversee that. Caleb was in charge of branding, and his days were so long, she often found him asleep on the couch when she'd go to visit him.

He showered her with affection and kicked her sexy smiles whenever he saw her around the ranch, but something lingered in an invisible space between them. He didn't bring up her graduate program again, and neither did she. She thought about it every day though, and though the deadline to apply loomed only a week away, she hadn't done so yet.

She'd been praying, and going to church every week even if Caleb couldn't come with her. She hadn't gone back to lunch with her parents yet, but the idea weighed heavily in her mind. Her old frustrations grew with every passing day that she didn't get an answer for what to do about graduate school. About Caleb.

Finally, with only two days until June first—the deadline to apply for the winter semester—she picked up the papers she'd had ready for weeks. The folder only held a few sheets of paper, but it seemed to weigh a hundred pounds.

Every limb felt heavy too as she walked over to Caleb's, glad the sun didn't set by four-thirty anymore. She knocked on his door and he called for her to come in. He poked his head around the fridge and lifted his hand in greeting. "I've got hot chocolate going."

Holly closed the door behind her, not quite sure why her stomach writhed so violently. She moved into the kitchen and watched Caleb as he moved around with ease. Within a few minutes, he had a plate of sandwiches on the table and mugs of hot chocolate and bags of chips.

"Those two are for you." He pointed to two sandwiches on the right.

"Thanks." She'd given up asking him how he came up with his concoctions, and in what universe had she ever eaten more than one sandwich? A smile flirted with her lips, but the folder in her fingers reminded her of what she needed to do.

"What's that?" he asked as he noticed the folder. "Did you get the hospital record?"

She shook her head. "No, I haven't tried again." She'd gone to the Gold Valley Hospital and asked to see the file for her father. The receptionist wouldn't give it to her. The best she could do was confirm that Darrel Gray had been seen in the emergency room only a day after Nathan had ended their engagement. That had been good enough for Holly—something had happened. Something bad enough to make her mother think they needed to go to the hospital. Caleb thought so as well, but he still wanted to see the file.

"So what's that?" He reached for a sandwich and took a bite, the loud crunch signaling that he'd put potato chips on his—again.

Holly took a deep breath and met his eye. "This is my graduate program application."

Caleb's eyes iced over, the only reaction Holly needed to know how he felt. "I see," he said. "When's that due?"

"Two days."

"You haven't done it yet?" He set his sandwich down, his attention on her almost unnerving.

"No." She looked at the folder as her eyes heated. She couldn't believe she felt like crying right now. Pushing the emotion away, she said, "I don't know what to do. I've been praying for an answer for weeks." Her shoulders lifted and fell, and those tears pressed in close, close, close. "I don't think I know how to get answers to my prayers." Holly lifted her chin and a tear trailed down her cheek.

Caleb left his seat and knelt in front of her, his strong hands cradling her face and wiping those tears. "Of course you do."

"No." She shook her head. "God doesn't answer me. He never has." She didn't want to get into all the particulars of why she believed that, so she smiled through her tears.

Caleb pulled her into an embrace and she relied on his strength because she had none of her own.

She'd told him she'd ignored his text the day he'd met Missy Bills. She'd ignored it, because she'd been praying to know how to answer him. And she hadn't gotten an answer then. She'd waited in his house for hours, praying for guidance, and strength, and that she would be wrong about what she'd seen and suspected. She didn't want to be the crazy, suspicious woman she'd been with Nathan. She *wasn't* that woman anymore, and she'd pleaded with the Lord to help her.

She had been wrong about what she'd seen, but she'd felt nothing from heaven. She honestly believed she didn't know how to feel on a spiritual level.

"What should I do?" she asked Caleb.

He pulled away, cleared his throat, and returned to his seat. "I can't tell you what to do." He looked at his sandwich but didn't pick it up.

"Caleb."

"I don't want you to go, okay?" He looked right at her, his eyes jumping with frustration. "I'm—I'm—I can't imagine my life without you, and…." He shook his head and sighed. "But just because I don't want you to go doesn't mean you shouldn't go." He stood, picked up a stack of sandwiches, his hot chocolate, and a bag of chips. "I'm gonna go eat with Ty." He left her sitting at his kitchen table, the application between them. Her forthcoming departure forever between them.

Holly watched him go, flinched when the front door

slammed behind him, and exhaled when she was finally alone.

"You wanted to do this program before you met him. Just apply. You might not get in, and you don't have to go if you do." She waited for a feeling of rightness to spread through her, the way it had that first day back at church. She felt nothing, so she spread out the papers, opened a PDF app on her phone, and snapped the pictures she needed. After she emailed them to herself, she left the food Caleb had prepared on his table and went back to her cabin so she could get her application done.

She moved slowly, methodically, so she could listen and feel for any indication that applying for her graduate program wasn't the right thing to do. With everything uploaded and filled out, all she had to do was hit submit.

Pausing, she closed her eyes and bowed her head. *Please,* she begged, a sense of desperation coating every cell in her body. *Please tell me what to do.*

Beyond her window, a bird chirped, its happy sound peaceful and comforting. She wasn't sure what the Lord was trying to tell her, but the almost frantic feeling in her chest subsided. She *breathed,* something she hadn't been able to do in weeks, and a single word entered her mind: *Trust.*

She opened her eyes and pushed the submit button. She could trust in her and Caleb. She could trust in the Lord.

"Whatever happens will happen," she whispered to herself. She moved her eyes to the ceiling. "Thank you."

# CHAPTER 18

A couple of weeks later, Holly drove to church with Caleb in her passenger seat. It was the first time in weeks he'd been able to go, and she flexed her fingers on the wheel. "I sent in my application," she said.

"I figured," he responded without looking at her.

She slid him a glance, but she couldn't read his expression. "It doesn't mean I'll get in."

He met her eyes and rolled his. "I'm sure you'll get in."

"Doesn't mean I'll go."

He shifted toward her. "And why would you apply if you weren't planning to go?"

She focused on her driving and lifted one shoulder in a shrug, all the answer she could come up with. "I can't believe there's still snow out here."

"It doesn't really disappear until July." His voice sounded strained and on the upper range of his pitch, but Holly didn't know what to do about it. "So there's a dance on

Friday in the valley," he continued. "Maybe you'd like to go with me."

Surprise shot through her as she rounded a bend in the canyon, almost down to the waterfalls. "You can get away from the ranch for a dance?"

"A bunch of boys go. Jace lets us off early if we work the weekends."

"This is something you've been doing for a while?"

"A few years, yeah." A cool note entered his tone, and Holly looked at him.

"You dance with a lot of girls?"

That sexy smile appeared on his face. "Only a few." He sobered a little, the smiling sliding away. "Haven't really been interested in women for a while."

Warmth and peace flowed through her, and her own smile couldn't be stopped. "You really think you're up to going back to my parents'?"

"Ready as I'll ever be." He sighed and flipped his phone over and over. "Maybe your dad will talk to me this time. Maybe we can get some answers from him."

"I wouldn't hold your breath," she said.

"Oh, come on." He chuckled. "I hold the record in Gold Valley for breath-holding. Won a contest a few years ago and everything."

She scoffed. "You did not."

"Did to. There was a contest at the fair, and I won. Held my breath for almost four minutes."

Holly tipped her head back and laughed at the pride in Caleb's voice. She pulled into the church parking lot, her carefree happiness still pulling through her. Caleb came around the truck and opened her door, leaning in to kiss her. In a rare moment of seriousness, he pressed his forehead to hers and whispered, "I hope you don't get into your program."

He pulled back so quickly, she wasn't sure if he'd actually spoken the words or not, but they lingered in her ears, wisped through her brain like smoke, and the pure emotion she heard in them chilled her.

With his hand extended toward her, she gripped his fingers and slid out of the truck. "I hope my dad talks to us today."

"Look who's praying for a miracle now." He bumped her to the side and chuckled as he pulled her back. They entered the church and paused in the doorway of the chapel.

"Hey," he said. "Maybe we should sit by them today."

She tipped her head back and looked at him. "I was just thinking the same thing."

Caleb took a deep breath, and Holly did the same, trying to steel herself for whatever may happen. Then she took the first step, Caleb right at her side.

———

Caleb applied a bit of extra pressure to Holly's back, and his intent to get her to stop was rewarded. She paused and looked at him. He chin-nodded toward a gaggle of women. Well, a gaggle to him was more than two, and as there were three eyeing them from a pew on the side, it qualified.

"They seem to want to talk to you," he murmured.

Holly painted a bright smile on her face and stepped over to her friends. She didn't relinquish her grip on Caleb's hand, so he went with her. Reluctantly, but he went. He lifted his free hand and touched his hat. "Mornin' ladies."

They twittered and in the past, a dose of satisfaction would've had him on a high for a few days—certainly long enough to get him back to the summer dance the next weekend. Now he just found the women standing in front of him a bit annoying.

Angie said something to Holly that Caleb didn't hear, because her mother had turned and was watching them. Caleb lifted his hand in greeting and gestured to them. Georgia's eyes widened, and she pointed to the bench next to her.

Caleb nodded and bent down to Holly. "I'm gonna go sit by your mom." He drifted away from her, his cowboy boots making too-loud thunking noises as he moved down the aisle.

"Morning, ma'am." He swiped his cowboy hat from his head and leaned over to give her a kiss on the cheek before he sat down, leaving room for Holly on the end of the bench.

"Good morning, Caleb." She straightened her shoulders, an air of importance around her. "We haven't seen you for weeks."

"I work a lot of Sundays," he said. He leaned forward and caught Darrel's eye. "Hullo, sir." He pasted a smile on his face, somehow trying to infuse extra friendliness into his voice and expression. "I hear we're coming to eat again this afternoon. I'm really happy about that."

"Why's that?" Darrel asked.

"Then I don't have to cook." Caleb leaned forward and lowered his voice to a conspiratorial whisper. "Since I don't get off the ranch much, it's nice to have someone cook for me for a change."

A flicker of a smile rushed through Darrel's eyes. "I'm sure my daughter doesn't help with that."

"She can't even boil water." Caleb chuckled. "I don't know how she made it out of your house, Georgia, without your supreme culinary skills."

Holly dropped onto the bench next to him and he leaned back. "Hey." He almost turned back to her parents, but the distress on her face made an alarm sound in his head. He twisted toward her and put his arm around her shoulders. "What's wrong?"

She raised her chin as it wobbled and shook her head. Her eyes were as hard as glass, and if she cried, Caleb knew she'd bolt. He looked helplessly at her and then her mother. "Holly's not feeling well," he whispered. "We'll be right back." He nudged Holly so she'd get up, but she remained stiff and unmoving.

"She's fine physically," Georgia whispered as the organ began playing. "One of those women said something to upset her."

Caleb peered down at the older woman. "How do you know that?"

"Because that was Angie Belnap, and she has a way of saying things that sound nice but that cut deep."

Caleb marveled at the ability of women to understand each other. He whispered, "Thanks, Georgia," and shifted back to Holly. "So what did Angie say?"

She finally swung her head toward him, but it seemed to happen in slow motion. She blinked, but the tears shining in her eyes didn't fall. Thankfully. With his free hand, he slipped his cowboy hat back on and leaned toward her until she was protected under the brim of it. "Come on, sunshine. What's wrong?"

"She said I must've really changed to still be with you."

The alarm in Caleb's head roared into overdrive. "What does that mean?"

"She said you like pretty women."

"Obviously." He grinned at her. "Is that a crime? And don't you want people to think you've changed?"

"I haven't changed."

"Holly, of course you have."

She shook her head much harder this time, and those blasted tears stained her cheeks. "You're wrong. I'm still paranoid and jealous. Did you really go out with her?" Before he could answer, she stood. "Never mind." She strode down the aisle right as Dr. Pinnion said, "Good morning, friends. What a beautiful summer day it is."

Holly's heels clicking on the wood faded, and Caleb remained in his seat, stunned and confused as to what had just happened. He didn't remember dating Angie Belnap, barely knew her in fact.

He glanced over his shoulder and found the honey-haired woman watching him. She grinned and waggled her fingers at him, troubling him even more. He definitely hadn't spoken to or seen the woman in at least three years.

What in the world was going on?

He wasn't sure, but something told him to stay in his seat, stay for the sermon, stay for lunch with Holly's parents. So he sent her a text, asking her to please come back inside, and then he tried to focus on what Dr. Pinnion said.

Such a feat was impossible, though, and Caleb found himself circling around what Angie could've said to Holly to make her so upset. The sermon finally ended, and Caleb felt like he'd been holding his breath for an hour. He exhaled as he stood, checking his phone for any response from Holly.

She'd told him that she'd ignored his text that day he'd met Missy, and it seemed like she was doing it again. He hated that, hated that she wouldn't talk to him, wouldn't at least let him know if he needed to find his own ride back up to the ranch.

"Are you coming over right now?" Georgia asked, and Caleb turned to her like she was his personal savior.

"Yes," he said. "Can I get a ride with you two? Holly left, and…." He trailed off, not sure how to finish the sentence as he scanned the chapel for her.

"I'm sure she'll meet us at the house." Georgia patted his arm as she slipped past him into the aisle. He followed her, but he was less sure that Holly would be waiting at her parents' house. No, she'd probably be brooding on his couch, waiting for him to show up so she could unleash her Latina anger on him when he finally showed up.

As hot as that made his blood run, he really just wanted her to stop acting…crazy. His thoughts kept his tongue quiet and his eyebrows drawn into a V. He sent a text to Holly: *I never went out with Angie,* and held his breath while her father navigated toward their house.

*Did you go back to the ranch? Should I be calling Jace or Ty for a ride?*

She still didn't answer, and her truck wasn't in her parents' driveway. Dread settled in Caleb's chest like a thick brick, but he had no choice but to go into the house with her mother and father. "Holly's not here," he said. "I can just call my boss for a ride."

"Nonsense," Georgia said, and Caleb appreciated her chipper voice. "You're hungry, so you'll eat first. Darrel, go light the grill and we'll get this chicken done." She bent herself into the fridge and pulled out a glass bowl with chicken marinading in soy sauce.

Caleb's stomach rumbled, and his mind tumbled, and his emotions jumbled. Darrel clapped him on the shoulder and said, "I might need some help lighting the grill."

Caleb figured that was as close to an invitation to go along with him as he was going to get, so he went. The screen door slammed behind him, causing Caleb to jump and focus. "Sorry."

"Don't be sorry, son." Darrel exhaled as he turned the knobs and stuck a long, gas lighter into the hole. One click and the grill lit—he certainly didn't need Caleb's help.

He turned toward Caleb, his blue eyes bright with what Caleb recognized as anxiety. "Holly asked me to talk to you about why I went to the emergency room."

Caleb's heart triple-beat, a little tap dance in his chest that didn't settle the way it would've had Holly simply been in the house with her mother, putting together a salad.

"You should know that it wasn't your father who hit me. Wasn't your father I went over to your house to see."

Every cell in Caleb's body felt like it had been hooked to an electric source, and energy now buzzed through him. He finally landed on the right person—the man who had hit Darrel Gray.

"It was Nathan." Caleb didn't even frame his words as a question.

Darrel nodded and smacked his lips. "Yep, it was Nathan. I didn't want Holly to know; she was in love with him for a long time after they broke up." He took a few steps past Caleb, moving to the railing on the deck. He stared out into the backyard, the garden that looked newly planted, the neat and trimmed apple trees. "And seein' you just reminded me so much of him."

"We are identical twins." Caleb stepped next to Holly's father and leaned his elbows on the railing, his own sigh slipping past his lips.

"Only in looks," Darrel said. "Everything else I've seen and heard from others is that you're nothing like Nathan."

A grin graced Caleb's face. "Finally, someone can see that." He cut a glance in Darrel's direction.

"Oh, I can see it." A ghost of a smile passed across

Darrel's face. "And I can also see my daughter is in love with you. I'm asking you not to hurt her."

Caleb blinked, reeling from the words *in love with you.* "Oh, Darrel." Caleb chuckled, but it sounded a lot like a bleating goat. "I think you're wrong. Holly and I—we're not quite that…serious." His voice trailed into silence. If he and Holly weren't serious, what were they? Why was he so worried about where she was? Why did he get angry and moody every time he thought of her leaving Gold Valley, leaving him?

Darrel chuckled too, his more carefree and casual. "Caleb, you better open your eyes before you miss what's standin' right in front of you." He turned and entered the house, the slamming screen door punctuating his statement in a profound way.

Caleb searched the empty yard, but he didn't see anyone or anything standing right in front of him—because Holly had walked out on him and now wouldn't answer his texts.

CHAPTER 19

Caleb climbed into Ty's truck, his nerves near raw after eating and conversing with Holly's parents without her. "Have you seen Holly?" he asked by way of greeting.

"Good afternoon," Ty said with a wry smile. "Nice to see you too. You're so welcome for driving forty minutes on a Sunday afternoon—the only one I've had off this month—to pick you up. Yes, I think we should drive through and get an ice cream cone." Ty flipped his truck into reverse and backed out of the driveway with a Cheshire Cat smile on his face.

Caleb rolled his eyes. "I've texted her a bunch of times. She won't answer me."

"Her truck was in her driveway when I left." Ty leveled his gaze at Caleb as he turned right. "She wouldn't answer the door when I knocked. I tried."

"But she's there."

"Was when I left."

A measure of Caleb's anxiety loosened, and his chest didn't feel smothered in ice and then encased in cement. Even though he scarfed a twist cone and sent his gratitude to the Lord when Ty passed the site of his accident, breathing was still hard.

The snow had long melted on the ranch, and the mud was mostly dry now too. Caleb liked the straight fence lines, and the well-maintained buildings. He felt like he was coming home when he pulled under the double-H arch of Horseshoe Home, and he relaxed further into his seat.

Upon rounding the corner, Ty said, "Uh oh," and Caleb jerked to attention. He saw Holly, and relief like he'd never felt rushed through him.

Then he noticed the box she carried. She placed it in the back of her truck and turned back to her cabin. Ty hadn't even come to a complete stop before Caleb jumped from the cab and ran toward Holly.

"Hey," he said breathlessly as he caught her at the base of the steps leading to her cabin. "What are you doing? Why haven't you texted me back?"

She turned her face away from him. "I don't belong on this ranch. I'm leaving."

Caleb's heart shriveled, and his muscles forgot how to move. She went up the steps and it wasn't until her footsteps muted that his brain caught up. He sprinted after her, leaving the front door swinging open.

Her hair hung like a dark curtain between them. She moved methodically, placing knick knacks and a couple of placemats in a box.

"Holly, I don't understand."

She lifted her head and glared, that fire he loved finally blazing through. "I hate Gold Valley," she said, her voice almost a hiss. "I hate it here, and I don't like the people here, and I don't fit in here. I never will. So I'm leaving."

"You don't like *any* of the people here?"

She deflated, but the heat in her eyes didn't extinguish. "Not all of them."

"Some of us are pretty great."

She shook her head, a tear falling to her cheek. "No one here will ever see me as anyone but Holly Gray, the drill team leader. Or Holly Gray, the woman who got dumped by Nathan Chamberlain and fled town." She went back to her packing, a sniffle sounding every few seconds.

Caleb sensed he was losing her, and fast. He advanced toward her, trying to keep her contained without spooking her, much like he would a horse. "Holly, who cares what they think?"

Her head jerked up. "I care, Caleb."

"I mean, obviously, you do. What I don't understand is *why* you care." He reached for her and slid his palms up and down her bare arms. The warmth of her skin teased him, but he pushed away the impulse to kiss her. "I don't know what Angie said. But it's not true. I didn't go out with her. Never wanted to. Never will." He bent his head so he was eye-level with her. "And I'm not sure why it matters to you who I may or may not have dated in the past. But you're the only one I want."

She seemed to soften, just for a moment. Then her resolve returned; her jaw clenched; she stepped back. "I'm still leaving." She ducked around him and strode to the front door. Turning, she surveyed the cabin. "I think that's all my stuff." She spun and was gone before Caleb could do or say anything.

He hadn't realized how personal she'd made her space. Though the remodel had turned the cabins into homes, she'd also added charm and personality with her snow globes and family pictures. He tore his eyes from the now-bare mantle and hurried after her.

He caught her as she set the box in the back and lifted the tailgate. "Come on," he said, putting his hand on it and almost yelping from the heat. He pulled away quickly. "You're not really just leaving, are you?"

She scanned the boxes in the back of her truck, scanned the surrounding ranch buildings and land, scanned his face. He wasn't sure what she saw there, but surely she could detect his utter desperation for her to stay.

Holly lifted onto her toes and pressed her lips to his in the sweetest kiss he'd ever had. He drank her in, nonverbally begging her to stay, pleading with her to come on over to his cabin while Ty took all her boxes back inside.

She pulled away, her tears staining his white church shirt and her words singeing his ears. "Yes, Caleb, I'm really leaving." And then she moved. Moved away from him. Moved into the cab of her truck. Moved on down the road.

Caleb stood in her driveway, mute and electrified, and watched. Watched the woman he thought he could love drive away. Watched as she took his whole heart with her, and the only thought in his head was how fast he could get down to the valley to buy a drink so he didn't have to feel so much at once.

Didn't have to feel at all.

———

Holly cried as she drove across the country. She paused for several minutes as she made important phone calls to line up somewhere to stay in Great Falls and to get a new job once she arrived back in Vermont.

By nightfall, she'd checked into her hotel, and even if she wasn't sure she'd be able to sleep because it faced the highway, she squared her shoulders. She had a phone, a credit card, and a truck. She could go anywhere, do anything.

She expected to feel as free and fresh as she had the first time she'd left Gold Valley, only a few weeks after Nathan had broken up with her.

But she didn't. A great weight seemed yoked to her neck, and no matter how many French fries she ate and no matter how loud she turned up the volume on the TV, she couldn't erase that last kiss with Caleb from her mind.

She heaved herself off the bed and took the few steps to the microwave to make hot chocolate. Though it was summer, and she certainly wasn't cold, a chill existed deep down inside her. She drank the liquid even though it scalded her tongue and throat, and that ice in her gut didn't soften, didn't warm.

"You can't go back," she told herself. She didn't like the person she was while in Gold Valley. She hadn't really believed Angie Belnap when she'd said Caleb had been coming around her place before Holly showed up. Caleb never left the ranch—he didn't want to leave the ranch—and that had become a real problem as she sat next to him in that chapel.

He loved the ranch, loved Gold Valley. And while she enjoyed her time on the ranch, with the horses and cows, the cowboys, with Caleb, she simply couldn't stay in Gold Valley.

Her old feelings of paranoia, or jealousy, of never being sure who she could believe and who she could trust, had roared to life since she'd seen Caleb sweep Missy into a hug outside the diner. She'd done her best to bury them, but in the end, she couldn't. There simply seemed to be something in the air in Gold Valley that made her crazy.

She sighed as she thought the word that had haunted her for months after Nathan had said it. Tears pricked the backs of her eyes and a sob wrenched itself from her throat as she flopped back onto the bed.

Half an hour later, she'd convinced herself she could text Caleb, just to let him know she was okay. He'd called twice and texted a half a dozen times since she'd left, all pleas for her to please come back and talk to him. They'd work through whatever Angie had said, and figure things out when she got into her program.

She appreciated that he'd said when and not if. She hated that she was the one hurting him, because she knew exactly how he felt.

"Not quite," she whispered into the pillow. He'd never said he loved her, and she'd never told him that. But the feelings were there, even if they hadn't bloomed all the way yet. She also knew his last girlfriend had walked out on him. Not for the same reasons, but the actions were the same, and Holly's misery doubled.

*I made it to a hotel,* she typed, careful not to tell him where she'd gone. While the idea of him roaring up in his old truck and stopping her from continuing her journey east appealed to her in a romantic way, she knew that would only postpone their breakup.

*I'm really sorry about today.* She stared at the message, thinking it might be natural to add *I love you* to the end of it, but also realized how incredibly unfair that would be. *Call me tomorrow?*

She wasn't sure she could stomach the sound of his voice, especially if he asked her to come back in that husky, throaty tone he used when he whispered how beautiful she was or how much he liked eating dinner with her. She hit send anyway, hoping he might actually be too busy to call.

*Can I call you now?* came his response in only seconds.

For the life of her, she couldn't think of a reason why he couldn't—other than her own volatile emotions.

*I promise I won't keep you awake past nine. It's been a long day for me, and—*

"Five o'clock comes early," Holly read the last part of his

text out loud, a lump lodging itself in her throat. She pressed her phone to her chest and stared helplessly at the flickering television. "What do I do?" Her gaze wandered heavenward, but she felt nothing.

Absolutely nothing.

# CHAPTER 20

$E$very frayed edge in Holly's chest soothed at the sound of Caleb's voice. Instead of begging her to get in her truck and come back, he told her about the church service she'd missed, dinner at her parents' house.

"So it was Nathan." Caleb sighed. "I haven't talked to him yet. Do you think I should call him?"

Holly pressed her eyes closed, wishing she could feel something about Nathan slugging her father. Maybe she simply couldn't feel at all anymore. Maybe it wasn't that God wasn't speaking to her, but that she'd completely forgotten how to do anything but breathe and blink.

*No*, she thought. She'd felt things for Caleb. She'd experienced joy with him, and heartache, and...love. She swallowed her emotions and said, "It's almost nine o'clock, so you'll probably have to wait until tomorrow to call him." She smiled at the ceiling, wishing she was only a short walk away from Caleb.

But she'd put miles of distance between them, and not just physically. She wasn't sure if she could ever go back to Gold Valley, and it didn't seem fair to keep talking to Caleb —who was never going to leave Gold Valley.

"I should go," she said, her voice rising in pitch. "I'll talk to you later."

He started to say something, but she spoke over him and then hung up before his protests could enter her ears. She curled her fingers around the phone, thinking the right thing to do would be to forget about Caleb Chamberlain. At the same time she determined to do just that, she knew she would never be able to push him completely from her mind. He seemed to have rooted himself there, for better or worse.

She thought about him as she tossed and turned. She dreamt of him as she slept. When she woke in the morning, packed her bag, and set her truck east again, he circled through her mind. He called, but she let it go to voicemail. If she did that enough times, would he stop calling? And why did that prospect make her heart feel ten sizes too small for her chest?

"*You* left." She slammed her palm against the steering wheel, startling herself. She glanced at herself in the rearview mirror, her dark eyes churning with fire. "*You* made a decision. Deal with it."

Deal she did. She arrived in Vermont a few days later, and because she hadn't burned any bridges in Island Park, she had an apartment waiting for her. A job she could start on Monday.

And a huge, cowboy-sized hole in her life.

Every day, that hole widened. She tried to stuff it with dark roast coffee and peanut butter sandwiches with potato chips. That would take the edge off for a couple of hours, and then she'd be near the verge of tears again.

At the beginning of August, she received the letter she'd been anticipating for years. With shaking fingers—and utterly alone—she ripped open the envelope. She pressed her eyes closed and inhaled deliberately. This wasn't how she'd imagined she'd open this letter. More and more lately, she'd pictured Caleb at her side, those milk chocolate eyes watching her with more than a little interest.

"Well, he's not here," she whispered. Her eyes popped open and in one motion, she lifted the flap on the envelope. Only a single sheet of paper sat inside, and it vibrated as she held it between her fingers. She unfolded it, her eyes already searching for the words she wanted to see.

*It is with great pleasure....*

A squeal erupted from Holly's mouth and she pressed the paper to her pulse. She'd gotten into the doctorate program. She held the letter out and kept reading to find out when her intern hours needed to be completed. She hadn't finished them before leaving Montana, and though she'd met with her old boss at Steeple Ridge, she hadn't earned nearly enough hours yet.

Sure enough, the third paragraph outlined that her intern hours needed to be completed by October thirty-first, and listed the amount needed. She didn't even have half of them.

She let the paper drop, and it fluttered to the counter. Her phone rang, making her jump out of her skin. She swiped it off the counter, half-hoping it would be Caleb. But in the six weeks she'd been gone, he'd stopped calling after the first two. He'd called everyday for two straight weeks— sometimes more than once a day. Then, apparently, her message had been received.

"Mom," Holly said. "Great timing." She smiled, glad she would be able to share this news with someone after all. Even if it wasn't the person she really wanted to.

"Holly," her mother started, and Holly knew she wouldn't be telling her mom about the veterinary acceptance. Her mother's tone suggested a lecture was coming, and Holly sank onto a barstool.

"What's going on, Mom?"

"I just ran into Caleb Chamberlain. That poor man." She clucked her tongue, no idea what her seemingly simple words had done to Holly's heartrate.

"What's wrong with him?" she asked, her voice barely more than air.

"He's heartbroken." Her mother sighed. "He looks like he hasn't slept since you left, and when he asked me about you, the hope in the man's eyes nearly killed me. Holly." Her mother's tone turned snappy and cold. "When are you going to come home and tell him you love him too? Well, maybe you should start with an apology, but—"

"Mom, I don't love him." Holly had told her mother this

repeatedly over the weeks. "And he doesn't love me." He'd never told her that, not in any of the voicemail messages he'd left, any of the texts he'd sent, before his radio silence.

"I may not know everything, but I know what heartbroken looks like."

"Mom." Holly rubbed her fingers across her forehead. "Anything else I need to know?"

"He mentioned that Horseshoe Home really needs a vet."

"I'm going to hang up now, Mom."

"Holly, he asked me where you were. Are you sure I can't tell him?"

"Yes, Mom," she said firmly. "I just…more time."

"More time for what?" Her mother's exasperation wasn't lost on her, but Holly couldn't articulate what she needed time to do in a way her mother could understand.

"Time to figure things out," she said. "I really have to go."

"All right. Daddy sends his love."

Holly said good-bye and hung up, her heart in constant turmoil with her brain. Her phone rang again, and Holly rolled her eyes as she swiped it on. "Mom," she started. "I mean it, I'm not—"

"I'm not your mother," a man said with a chuckle in his voice.

Pure horror raced through her, making her skin feel like someone had dunked her in a tank of ice water. She pulled the phone from her ear and looked at it, almost desperate for it to be anyone but Caleb.

A the same time, she really wanted it to be Caleb.

"Jace," she breathed. "I'm sorry, my mother had just

called, and—" She clamped her lips shut. "What can I do for you?"

"I need you back on the ranch," he said.

Holly flinched like she'd been slapped. "Well, that's blunt."

"I don't have a lot of time." He chuckled. "Sorry. But we've got half our cow-calves down with pinkeye, and there's some sort of hoof rot thing going on." He paused and exhaled. "I need you, Holly. Even just for a few weeks. Caleb said your, uh…." He cleared his throat. "He said you wouldn't be starting school until at least January, and I could really use your help. Cabin's still here, and it won't snow until the beginning of October. That's two months. I know you hate the snow."

Holly had never heard the foreman say so much at once. She had heard the emotion in his voice—pure desperation. She understood how he felt. Every cell in her body wanted to return to Horseshoe Home. She glanced at the letter lying on the counter. Just lying there.

She didn't even have half of the required intern hours. Would she even be able to get them all? What if she couldn't? Then what would she do? Working at the boarding farm was great and all, but it wasn't what she wanted to do for the rest of her life.

"I need to sleep on it," she said.

"Fair enough," Jace said. "I'll have my phone with me all day tomorrow. Call anytime."

Holly nodded, though Jace couldn't see her. "Jace, um, how's Caleb?"

The foreman sighed again. "He's about how you're imagining, Holly. I'll talk to you later." He hung up, and Holly stared at her phone.

In her imagination, Caleb wasn't doing well at all. She knew, because she wouldn't be had she been in his position. In fact, she wasn't doing well at all and *she* was the one who'd chosen to leave.

Frustrated, and with that letter practically mocking her, Holly retreated to her bedroom. She switched on the television, changed into her pajamas, and climbed into bed. After a half an hour, she hadn't really seen a single minute of the movie playing as consumed with her future as she was.

She slipped from under her comforter and knelt next to the bed. She took a deep breath and bowed her head. Though she felt like she'd never really gotten an answer, she had been trying to trust herself. Trust God.

"Dear Lord," she started, her prayer quickly turning silent. Words streamed through her head as she poured her whole heart and soul into her pleadings with the Lord. Spent, she dragged herself back into bed, her tears making the pillow slightly damp.

As the TV flickered in the darkness, Holly listened. But for the first time, she listened to her heart more than anything else.

And her heart wanted her to go back to Gold Valley. She felt asleep still undecided, but with fantasies of what her life could be like...with Caleb.

Caleb banged his palm against the stable door to get it to open. He stomped away from the building and kept right on going. His patience—with himself, with the other cowboys, with the horses—was at an all-time low. He'd learned over the past couple of months to walk away when he wanted to punch something.

Once he got out into the open fields, there wouldn't be anything to punch and that would be the safest place for all involved. He groaned as he tipped his head back and stared into the clear blue sky. August in Montana was his favorite time of year, and he felt it slipping through his fingers like smoke.

With sick cattle and a new, mouthy cowboy on-staff, Caleb woke with a headache and ate with a headache and went to bed with a headache. He'd been down to the valley twice since Holly had left town; once to go to church with her parents, and once to mope around his sister's apartment after she'd cut his hair.

He called Katie almost every night, just to complain to her about life on the ranch. Last night, she'd said, "Caleb, if you're so unhappy there, why don't you quit? Do something else?"

He didn't even know what else he would do. He knew horses, and building fences, and repairing farm equipment. He knew cattle, and planting, and branding, and winter weather. He'd said, "Katie, I'm not really unhappy. I just need a safe place to vent. Jace is tired of listenin' to me."

"He is not," she said. "He's tired of listening to you

complain about the ranch when you're really complaining about—"

Caleb heard what she hadn't said, so he said it. "Holly."

"She's still not answering her phone?"

"I think she probably blocked my number," Caleb growled. "I haven't tried in a long time anyway."

"You're still talking to her parents, though, right?"

"Every week."

"What do they say?"

The frustration he'd endured for almost two months reared up, choking him. Sometimes he could control it, push the anxiety back where it belonged—in his boots. Today, he didn't have the energy. So his dissatisfaction with his life spilled out. His fists clenched and his teeth ground together.

He knew what would come next: his old friend desperation. He housed a well of it so deep, it sometimes drowned him if he let in just a little bit. It surged up his throat, and his stomach coiled until it was so tight, his muscles screamed for a release.

"Why did she leave?" he asked no one. He'd asked over and over and he'd never found a satisfactory answer. "How long do I have to feel like this?"

When Robin had left, Caleb hadn't dealt with his emotions. He'd drunk them away. But he wouldn't do that again, though he considered it every single day. He shifted his weight, a slight pain in his leg reminding him of the consequences of letting even a drop of whiskey back into his life.

The clippity-clop of horse's hooves made him turn to find Jace riding up on his horse. "Not in the mood, Jace." Caleb turned away from his best friend, his frustration hardening into anger.

Jace dismounted and joined Caleb. For once he didn't try to explain that Holly probably just needed a little bit of time. Caleb had heard all about Jace's relationship with Belle. How he'd shown up on her doorstep one night and practically demanded she marry him. How he'd gone into a tailspin and he just needed time to confront his demons.

Even Belle had told Caleb her side of the story. If he heard her say, "Be patient," one more time, Caleb thought he'd self-combust.

"Ty and Will said you left in a hurry," Jace finally said.

"I don't know what else to do with the calves," he said. "I just needed a minute."

"Yeah, sure." Jace let the breeze whisper around them again. "You gonna go down to the dance tonight?"

"I don't see why I should." Caleb glanced at Jace. "Did Ty send you up here to get me to go?" Ty had been relentless about getting Caleb down to the summer dances. He still hadn't gone, but Ty was like a shark and he could smell blood in the water. He'd been wearing Caleb down for weeks, and just like Caleb didn't have the energy to contain his emotions, he couldn't keep arguing with Ty either.

"No, he didn't. I was just askin'."

"I need a drink." Caleb could barely swallow, and the words scraped against the back of his tongue.

"Nope." Jace turned Caleb around and pointed back to

the stable. "No, you don't. What you need is to get on down to the dance tonight. Get off this ranch. Remember there's a world out there."

"Jace."

"I hired a new vet," Jace said. "So you don't need to worry about the calves anymore."

Caleb's feet grew roots and he stared at Jace. "You hired a new vet?"

Jace rocked back on his heels, a proud smile on his face as he tucked his hands in his jeans pockets. "Sure did."

"How—who—?" Caleb couldn't get himself to form a complete sentence. He wanted a veterinarian on-staff at Horseshoe Home. But he wanted the vet to be Holly, and if Jace had hired someone else, she could never come back.

*She's never coming back anyway*, he thought, and he tore his eyes from Jace's. Bitterness burned in his mouth, and he started back to the stables, just as furious as he'd been when he'd left.

———

"I can't believe I'm doing this," Caleb grumbled later that night.

"Come on, man." Ty slapped Caleb's shoulder before he climbed in the truck Will was driving. "The dances are fun, and summer's almost over."

"What's fun about them?"

"There's ice cream, for one," Will said.

"It's not the ranch," Ty added.

"I like the ranch." Caleb got in the truck and slammed the door behind him.

"You're miserable on that ranch." Ty fiddled with the radio. "This will be good for you."

"Vegetables are good for me too, and I don't like those."

Will laughed but Ty just rolled his eyes. "You don't have to date someone. Just ask someone to dance, and eat some ice cream, and try to relax."

Caleb turned his attention out the window instead of answering Ty. He didn't want to dance with a woman. Not when he wasn't over Holly. As they rounded corner after corner and left the canyon, Caleb wondered if he'd ever be over her. Right now, it didn't feel like that would ever happen.

With a jolt like lightning, he realized he was in love with Holly Gray. All the way, deep down, in love with her.

"I love her," he blurted, looking at his friends in the truck.

"No kidding?" Ty asked in a highly sarcastic voice. "I had no idea." He turned to Will. "Will, did you know Caleb is in love with Holly?"

"Yeah, sure," Will said with a shrug. "Everyone knows."

Caleb stared at Ty and Will. "Wait, what?"

Ty elbowed him. "It's so obvious you're in love with her. It's been obvious for months."

Caleb shook his head, a scoff escaping as a flush rose into his face. "Stop foolin' around."

"I'm not," Ty said. "What? You think we didn't notice you cooking her dinner every night? Going to church with her?

Kissing her in the stables, the barns, out in the open?" He laughed, the sound filling the cab as Will approached the spot where Caleb offered up his prayer of gratitude. "I've never seen you so enamored with a girl before, and we've been friends forever."

"I—I—"

"Love her," Ty said. "You don't need to be embarrassed about it."

Caleb rubbed his hands over his face. "What am I gonna do now?" He didn't normally let Ty and Will see this vulnerable side of him. He saved that for Jace and Belle, for Katie. "Should I go to Vermont or something?" He suddenly felt frantic, like he needed to get out of this truck and do something.

Ty's guffaw nearly deafened Caleb. "No, you can't go traipsing off to Vermont." He exchanged a glance with Will. "It's almost the harvest. Don't worry so much. When Holly realizes how much she loves you too, she'll come back." Ty spoke with such confidence, Caleb was almost convinced that she'd come back to Gold Valley, to him.

*Almost* convinced.

Caleb arrived late to the staff meeting on Monday morning, his emotional turmoil not preventing him from sleeping. After the dance on Saturday night, he'd put in a full day of work around the ranch before going to Katie's for dinner. He'd stayed later than he should've, mostly because it felt nice to not be alone in his cabin. He hadn't realized how much life Holly had infused into his space simply by being there. Now he hated being alone in his cabin.

"Sorry," he mumbled to Jace, who shot him a glare.

"Now that we're all here, I have the weekly assignments. They need to be done today or tomorrow, in addition to your daily chores." He moved around the room and called names and matched them with assignments. Caleb stayed slumped in his seat, not listening until Jace called his name.

He lifted his eyes to the boss. "Groceries. And that has to be done today, cowboy." He handed Caleb a list. "Boys, get your requests to Caleb by ten o'clock so he can get down to the valley and back by dinnertime."

"I'm going alone?" he asked, glancing at the two-page list of groceries Jace wanted.

"I can't spare anyone else." Jace wouldn't look at him, and Caleb's suspicions shot through the roof. He waited until Jace finished handing out the assignments, until he went over the problems the ranch was currently having and what they could do about them, until all the other boys were through the door and onto their assignments.

"What's goin' on?" he asked as Jace tried to escape down the hall to his office.

"Nothing." Jace kept walking. "I have paperwork. It's almost the end of the month."

"Why do I have to do the grocery shopping alone? You never send one person alone." He followed Jace into his office and leaned against the doorjamb.

Jace sat heavily behind his desk. "Look, I need you to get all the groceries, yes. And I need you to pick up the new vet and bring her up here."

Whatever Caleb had been thinking, it wasn't that. "Her?" he choked out. "I'm not going to be interested in another vet, boss."

Jace flashed a brief smile. "That's not why I'm sending you."

"Good, because I'm, well, I've decided to follow your advice." He lifted his chin, almost in defiance. "I'm going to be patient. I think Holly will come back."

Jace nodded, a glimmer of light in his eyes. "Good for you, Caleb."

"So why do I have to meet this new vet?"

"You like the grocery shopping, and you know the most about our cattle. I figured I was doing you a favor."

Caleb narrowed his eyes. "You trying to get me off the ranch for some reason?" He folded his arms. "It's not even my birthday."

"January," Jace said. "I know. And yes, you need to get off this ranch more often."

"I've been down to the valley twice in the past two days."

"Great." Jace pulled a folder toward him. "Today will make three times. Now go on. Looks like you have quite a lot to buy." He nodded to the fistful of papers Caleb had clenched in his fingers. "The vet will meet you at the grocer. She'll be getting her own stuff, so leave her some room in the back of your truck."

"Yeah, yeah." Caleb pushed away from the wall and walked to his truck, sure he'd have to take three trips through the grocery store to get everything.

Caleb took a few minutes to organize the list, figuring he could sort it all back at the ranch. But if he was going to have to load an entire cart of groceries in his truck and go back for more, he couldn't have his precious vanilla bean ice cream melting while he picked up Ty's sweet onion chips, now could he?

He got canned goods and packaged foods first. Nothing frozen or fresh, and loaded all the brown paper sacks into the back of his truck before covering them with a tarp and heading back inside for diary, produce, frozen, and meat. He had his doubts that he could get all of that into one cart, but he was sure going to try.

No one stood out to him in the store. Everyone he saw, he knew. Had known his whole life. Gold Valley didn't attract a lot of outsiders, and he wondered who this new vet Jace had hired was. Where they were coming from. Why they'd come to Gold Valley.

With only a few items left on his list—and no shenanigans this time—a woman called his name. A powerful sense of déjà vu swept over him, and he prolonged the moment until he turned.

It couldn't be Holly….

He twisted, not fully committing to turning all the way around, especially if it was someone he didn't want to see or talk to. Katie beamed at him as she strode down the aisle, a gallon of milk in her hands.

Relief bloomed though him and a smile danced across his face. "Hey." He swept Katie into a sideways hug and squeezed her shoulders. "Just milk today?" She didn't even have a cart.

"Just helping a friend shop," she said, pointing back over her shoulder. "She forgot something over in the bakery. Something about chocolate caramel covered pretzels."

Caleb followed the way she'd pointed, searching for someone he probably wouldn't be able to locate. "I like those too," he said. "I'm just picking up the groceries for the ranch."

Katie eyed his overflowing cart. "I can see that. I hope you're almost done."

"Just a few more things," he said. "I think I can fit them."

"You wanna come meet my friend?" Katie cocked her head and hooked her thumb over her shoulder. "She's new in town and could stand to make a few friends."

Everything inside Caleb groaned. "Nah, I have to go."

"Come on." Katie pulled on his hand and started walking backward. "It'll take two seconds."

"Katie, I'm not interested—"

"So because Holly left town, you're going to go on another five-year dating hiatus?"

"Yes," Caleb said. "That sounds about right." He pulled his hand away. "I'm—I'm not over her, and I don't want to rush getting over her. I'm not interested in your friend. If she knows you, she won't have any problem meeting lots of other people." He returned to his cart and glanced at his list.

"Okay, well, see you later."

Caleb lifted his hand in acknowledgement and put his back into getting his cart moving toward the frozen juice. If he could get that, a lasagna, and a few boxes of waffles, he could get out of here.

He balanced the cans of juice precariously near the front of the cart and started loading waffles toward the back. He glanced back down the aisle when someone said, "No, there has to be pumpkin spice creamer."

Two women had stopped halfway down the aisle. Katie was one of them, and she held two bottles of coffee creamer in her arms. "There wasn't. It's only August."

The dark haired woman turned fully around, but Caleb would know her anywhere. "Holly?" ghosted from his lips.

She didn't turn, of course. His whispered words had barely registered in his ears. He abandoned his cart completely, his cowboy boots almost slipping as he nearly ran down the aisle. He bypassed Katie and called, "Holly!"

She turned, and Caleb stalled at the beautiful sight of her. He stared at her, a case of butter and sour cream between them. Her eyes harbored a knowing look and they danced with an emotion he couldn't name.

Heck, he couldn't even remember his own name at the moment. All he could hear was the thundering of his pulse in his chest, in his mouth, in his ears.

"Are you just gonna stand there and stare at her?" Katie sidled up beside him and nudged him with her elbow. "Go give her a kiss hello."

Kissing had been on Caleb's mind, and his sister's encouragement was all he needed to set his feet in motion. He ran toward the case, and vaulted it, landing just a few feet from Holly.

"You could've just gone around," she teased.

"What are you doing here?" He willed her to say she'd moved back, that she couldn't bear to be away from him for another minute.

"I'm starting a new job."

Caleb took a step closer to her, his gaze dropping to her mouth and lifting back to her eyes. "Oh yeah?" He reached for her hands, and gently threaded his fingers through hers. All the parts of him that had been coiled tight since she left released. He sighed and closed his eyes as he breathed in the soft strawberry scent of her hair. "I miss you so much."

"Good thing I took that veterinary job at the ranch, then."

Caleb flinched like he'd been punched and he leaned back to look at Holly. "Are you serious?"

"Very." She tipped up onto her toes, her mouth getting dangerously close to his. "And I can't survive up there without my coffee creamer."

Caleb chuckled and lifted his hands to her face. "I love you, Holly." He studied her as surprise melted into pure desire.

"I love you too, Caleb."

He grinned for a moment before going in for the kiss he'd been missing for the past two months.

———

Holly hadn't realized how much she'd missed Caleb. She thought she'd understood the level of isolation she'd achieved. She had underestimated it. She thought she'd be able to live without him. She'd been wrong.

"I love you," he said again, his lips catching against hers. "I'm over the moon you came back." He laughed as he lifted her off her feet and swung her around, his cowboy hat falling off. All at once, he sobered. "Wait a minute. Does Jace know you're coming back?"

She giggled and found her feet before saying, "He better. He said he'd have my cabin ready."

Caleb chuckled as he shook his head and picked up his hat. "So I'm the last one to know you're back, is that it?" He reached for her precious pumpkin spice creamer and handed it to her, a measure of challenge in his expression.

"I wasn't sure how you were feeling." She backed up against her cart. "I wasn't sure if you'd be happy to see me or not."

"Of course I'm happy to see you. I called you for weeks after you left." He edged closer to her, and she just wanted him to kiss her again. "I just told my sister I wasn't over you, and now that you're here, I'm not sure I could ever get over you." He put both his hands on the handle of the shopping cart behind her, trapping her close to her body. "You're not going to leave again, are you?"

She shook her head, struck by his handsomeness, the delicious scent of his cologne. "I got into my program, but only if I could get the intern hours done. I didn't have them complete, and I realized I didn't want to do them. Jace called me the next day." Tears she hadn't anticipated sprang to her eyes. "I prayed about it, and Caleb, I got an answer." She smiled up at him. "So here I am."

"I'm so glad." He touched his mouth to hers. "That you got an answer to your prayers." He trailed his lips along her jaw, and she shivered with the desire to be with him for the rest of her life. "That you're back." He formed his mouth to hers and kissed her. Kissed her like he'd never kissed her before.

"All right," Katie said from somewhere outside Holly's reality. "People are starting to stare."

Caleb broke their connection, but he didn't step back. Holly's head swam and she couldn't do much more than smile. Katie elbowed him, and he released the cart and backed up, ducking his chin so that his cowboy hat concealed his eyes.

"And all your juice is melting," Katie said. "Go get your cart. And you." She rounded on Holly, her eyes alight with laughter though her voice sounded harsh. "You got your pumpkin spice creamer, so it's time to go."

"Yes, ma'am," Holly said, which caused Caleb to chuckle. She hadn't realized how much she'd missed hearing his voice, smelling his skin, simply being with him. She realized it now, and she thanked the Lord that He'd prompted her to return to Gold Valley right when she wanted to be here.

———

A few days later, Caleb found her in the stable, bent over as she examined the back hoof of a horse that had started limping. "Hey." He leaned against the railing, so sexy Holly's breath whooshed out of her lungs.

"Hey, yourself." She straightened and moved toward him to get her kiss. "What are you doing here?"

"I came to ask if you wanted to go down to the summer dance tonight."

"Me and you?"

"Yeah, me and you." He chuckled. "Who else do you think I'm in love with?" He shook his head, but his smile indicated he wasn't really serious. "I thought we could go to dinner beforehand, go dancing, get some ice cream or something after."

"Well, as long as there's ice cream after."

"Go fix that horse."

"You go check your crops, then."

"Fine, I will."

"Fine, then I'll 'fix' this horse."

He took a few steps away and turned back. "Six o'clock okay?"

"Just fine." She returned to her work, a giddiness in her chest she hadn't experienced before. She was going down to dinner with her parents the following evening, and she wondered if she should invite Caleb to come with her. She felt like she needed to talk to them without him, tell them she was in love with him and hoped to marry him, find out if her father was okay with that.

She wasn't sure what she'd do if he wasn't. Since she'd been back, she'd realized that she'd lost two months of her life. Sure, she'd lived, but she hadn't *lived*.

By six o'clock, she'd "fixed" the horse, showered, and slipped into a little red dress she knew made her skin look more exotic and her hair shine like black gold. She's just stepped into a pair of shiny black heels when Caleb knocked and then pushed open her cabin door.

He whistled when he saw her and he pulled her close for a kiss. "I like what you've done with the place."

"You didn't even look at it."

"Yeah, the snow globes on the mantle are nice."

She batted playfully at his chest. "Stop it." She giggled

when his fingers slid along her sides and the teasing heat in his eyes intensified.

"Where'd you get the flowers?"

"Gloria lets me come cut her roses back for her." Holly turned toward the kitchen table, where she'd displayed the multi-colored blooms. "They're pretty, right?"

"Mm, pretty." He inhaled, his face tucked close to her neck. "So, are you ready?"

She stepped out of his embrace and plucked her purse from its spot on the counter. "Yes, ready."

The conversation was easy and light on the way to dinner, but a tremor of anxiety pulled through her when Caleb pulled into the best Italian restaurant in town, Migliano's. "Wow," she said. "I'm glad I wore a dress." She scanned him in his dark jeans, cowboy boots, and blue button-up shirt. "I should've known, what with you abandoning your plaid."

He glanced down at his clothes. "I like plaid."

"Oh, I know," she said as he opened his door and let in the summer heat. She slid out after him, enjoying the warmth from his touch and suddenly anticipating the taste of garlic bread and marinara sauce.

They were seated immediately, because Caleb had a reservation. Holly was impressed by his attention to all the little details, even waiting until she sat before he did. When he looked at her again, she found panic on his face.

"What?" she asked.

He glanced around the busy restaurant and cleared his

throat. The waiter came over and said, "My name is Justin. What can I get you to drink?"

Caleb managed to answer him, but once he'd left, Caleb turned mute again. Holly tried to strike up a conversation about her parents, but it wasn't exactly the lightest topic. The waiter returned with their sodas, and Caleb visibly relaxed.

"Here's your bread." Justin fumbled the basket, but managed to get it on the table. Caleb lunged for it while Holly asked for a straw. The waiter patted his apron pockets and finally came up with one. By the time Holly looked back to Caleb, he'd eaten most of his bread.

"Didn't you eat your pre-dinner snack?" She swirled her straw in her cola before taking a sip.

"I want to ask you something," he said.

She put her elbows on the table and leaned into them. "All right."

In one fluid movement, he oozed from his seat and knelt next to her. "Will you marry me?" The cracking of the ring box lid sounded like a gunshot, and every noise in the restaurant dimmed.

She stared first at him, and then the diamond glittering in the black box in his hand. Her heart leapt against her breastbone, and she pressed her hand over her pulse to calm it.

Caleb looked at her with such hope, such adoration, and she felt the same about him. She reached out, swept one hand down the side of his face, and said, "Yes."

whole colony of angry ants had taken up residence in Holly's chest. They swam through her bloodstream and crawled along her skin. She didn't regret her engagement to Caleb. That had been the happiest moment of her life.

Her father had taken the news well, and her mother had shed tears of joy. The wedding preparations had gone without a hitch. With only two days to spare until the big event, Holly woke with the insects everywhere.

She recognized her panic and tried to smother it. She knew why she felt this way—Nathan. Nathan was coming into town today with his wife and child.

She and Caleb had talked about this particular situation dozens of times over the past several months. Caleb had called and spoken to Nathan several times. First about the altercation with Holly's father. Then about the engagement. Caleb claimed that his brother was fine with it. He'd admitted to slugging her father, said he'd regretted it everyday since.

But Holly still had to face him and his wife at her own wedding. She had to look right into their faces and forgive them. She'd started that process with Nathan, and she was determined to finish it. The prickles cascading over her intensified as she thought about facing Mel. About forgiving her for perpetuating an inappropriate relationship. Whether she and Nathan had done anything physical during Nathan's previous engagement or not, they *had* developed an emotional relationship that shouldn't have been fed.

Holly swallowed and forced herself to sit up. She was going to be Nathan's sister-in-law. If she wanted to be Caleb's wife—and she did—she'd have to see Nathan and Mel a lot more over the years. She'd have to send their children birthday cards and money folded into little animals. She'd probably take her children to Nathan so he could fix their teeth, as it had always been Nathan's dream to come back to Gold Valley and open a practice in town.

She needed to figure out how to forgive Mel, and fast. Once again, she'd spent weeks and months praying without results. But she knew she'd get the words she needed, when she needed them. God had shown her that He was there, and just because He didn't speak loudly to her didn't mean He wasn't there at all.

Someone knocked, and she assumed it to be Caleb, so she called, "Come in," as she pushed off the covers and got out of bed. She went to the door and glanced into her living room.

"You're not even dressed," Caleb said when he spotted her.

"We're not leaving for an hour." She finger-combed her hair and stayed put because she still had morning breath. "What are you doing here so early?"

"I'm always up early. This is 'late' morning."

She laughed. "Well, I'm going to shower. Maybe you can make me breakfast or something."

He snorted and laid his head against the back of the couch before closing his eyes. "I'll see what I can whip up."

She went through her morning routine, paying special attention to her hair and makeup. She wasn't trying to impress anyone; she just wanted to feel confident when she had to face Mel and Nathan in just a few short hours. Thankfully, she just had to make it through lunch in Great Falls and then the drive home.

She and Caleb had already planned to grab fried chicken and eat dinner at the waterfalls after they dropped Mel and Nathan at Caleb's parents' house. "To decompress," Caleb had said. "There's nothing better than fried food."

"And biscuits," Holly had said. She smiled at her reflection as she remembered Caleb's chuckle, the tender way he kissed her, kneaded her closer, and promised her everything would work out.

She left the safety of her bedroom to find Caleb standing in the kitchen, buttering toast. "I couldn't do more than this," he said.

Plucking a slice from the stack, she said, "Wow, you're really off your game. I thought I got to be the nervous one today."

"I'm not nervous. It's going to be fine."

"Then why couldn't you manage more than toast?"

"Because what I'd make for breakfast, you wouldn't eat." He bit into a piece of toast and grinned. "I figured this was safe." He polished off his breakfast in record time and studied her as she nibbled around the edge of her piece of bread. "Nathan's going to be nice. You know that, right?"

"I'm not worried about him being nice." Holly pushed away her toast and stood to find her shoes.

"You're going to be able to forgive her." Caleb stepped into her path and gazed down at her.

"I'm going to try." Holly leaned toward him and he gathered her close, closer. "I really am going to try."

The four-hour drive to the airport passed in a blink. Holly couldn't remember a single country song they listened to, or a single word of conversation between them. She started out feeling fine, strong even. But as the city came into sight, that nest of ants seemed to stir, surge, swarm.

As she walked with Caleb toward baggage claim, she thought sure she should jump on the next flight out of town and never come back. But she'd done that twice now, and her happiness didn't exist outside of Gold Valley. It never had—something she knew now.

Soon enough, Nathan's flight number appeared on a carousel, and within a few minutes, Holly spotted him walking toward them. He was hard to miss with his height and all. She stiffened for a moment, and then a flood of understanding hit her.

She'd been looking into Nathan's face everyday for almost a year. The sight of him was nothing, meant nothing, stirred nothing inside her.

Caleb squeezed her hand and pulled her forward. He chuckled as he embraced his brother and murmured something Holly didn't catch. As she watched them, she realized how utterly different they were. Sure, they looked the same on the outside, but Caleb wore that cowboy hat every waking second, and Nathan's hair was styled to the side. He wore a casual polo and slacks—to fly in. Caleb didn't own anything but jeans, and he even wore those to church.

"Let me take him." Caleb took his nephew from Nathan and returned to Holly's side. "You remember Holly Gray." He beamed at her.

"Holly." Nathan smiled at her and engulfed her in a hug she thought should feel awkward, but somehow didn't. Peace flowed through her as she hugged him back, as he said, "I'm so happy for you." He pulled back a little, but left his hands on her shoulders. "You know that, right? Just because I couldn't make you happy doesn't mean I don't want you to be happy." He slid a devilish look at his brother as his words sunk into Holly's soul. "I just can't believe this guy makes you happy."

"Hey," Caleb said. "I finally found someone who appreciates my jokes."

"Some of them *are* good," Holly said, a genuine smile gracing her face.

"*Some* of them?" Caleb asked as Nathan returned to Mel's side. Holly marveled at how easily she'd forgiven him, how deeply his words had touched her, how she no longer held any vitriol toward him at all.

She glanced at Mel, her throat a sticky mess. All at once, Holly realized she'd heaped all the blame for her failed relationship with Nathan on Mel. Warranted or not, she needed to get over it.

"Mel, have you ever met Holly?" Nathan glanced back and forth between them, his nervous energy obvious.

"I don't think so," the woman chirped. She wore a sundress—she'd freeze before they made it back to the truck. Just because it was April didn't mean it was warm—and her straw-colored hair back on the sides. She glanced at the toddler Caleb still held, her eyes zooming away from Holly's and back again.

"Nice to meet you," Holly forced through stiff lips. She held out her hand and shook Mel's, only a fraction of the forgiveness she'd given Nathan streaming through her.

*So it will just take more time,* she thought. "What's your son's name?"

"Eddie." Mel smiled at him, her love for the little boy obvious. "And we're having another one in October."

"That right?" Caleb said, his gaze also dancing to Holly and back to his brother. "Well, congratulations."

"We hope to be back in Gold Valley by then," Nathan said. "All I need to do is pass my clinical here in Montana.

I'm doing it next week while we're here." Nathan slung his arm around Caleb and they turned toward the baggage carousel as it started spiting out luggage. "Good thing you chose April to get married."

"Give that credit to Holly. I would've married her last fall, but she wanted a spring wedding."

Holly hung back and watched Caleb and Nathan, her heart swelling with love for her soon-to-be cowboy husband. Eddie fussed a little, and Caleb soothed him quickly with a small sucker from his pocket.

Tears came to her eyes. Happy tears, because she was finally getting everything she'd always wanted. Maybe not when she wanted it, and with who she'd thought she wanted it with.

*Thank you for allowing me a chance to trust you.* She took a deep breath as she closed her eyes, her gratitude to the Lord for His guidance—even if He was still mostly silent with her —overwhelming and wonderful.

"Thank you for being nice to me," Mel whispered, and Holly startled away from her voice. She hadn't even realized how close Mel had wandered. She blinked at her, unsure of what to say. "You didn't have to be, and if I was you, I probably wouldn't have been." A small smile crossed the other woman's face.

"I—I—" Holly clamped her lips shut. She hadn't known what to expect from Mel, but it wasn't an apology. In her mind, Mel was a horrible person who stole fiancés. But as she looked at her now, she saw more than that. A lot more.

She saw another child of God, and her heart toward Mel softened.

"Anyway, thank you." She stepped forward to take her son as Caleb and Nathan lifted the luggage they wanted from the belt. Holly felt a bit removed from her reality, like a slip of plastic wrap hovered between her and everyone else in the airport. Even the chatter and noise sounded muted.

Then Caleb punctured the bubble and said, "Well, I'm starving. Should we go to lunch?"

Holly tucked her hand in his, her strength, her rock, her everything. He looked down at her, saw something in her eyes, and leaned over to kiss her. "Love you," he whispered, doing and saying everything she needed to be whole.

———

Caleb knew whoever stood on the other side of his front door was unfamiliar with how things worked at Horseshoe Home. People knocked and then entered. But this person had knocked and waited.

He opened the door to find his brother standing on the porch. If there was someone who didn't belong on a ranch, it was Nathan with his suit pressed into neat lines, his shirt so white it almost blinded Caleb, and that hair swept to the side like he spent his free time surfing.

"Morning." Nathan smiled as he entered Caleb's cabin. He drank in the walls, the couch, the small kitchen to the right. "This is nice, Caleb."

"It works," Caleb said. "Holly brings over the flowers." He admired the vase resting on his mantle, filled with peach and pink roses.

"So you'll live here after you're married?"

"That's the plan." He nodded to the hat box in his brother's hands. "What's that?"

"Mel and I wanted to get you something for the ceremony." He lifted the lid to reveal a silver felt hat that made Caleb suck in a breath.

"Nathan," he murmured. "You can't afford a hat like that." He raised his eyes to his twin's.

Nathan's eyes danced with excitement. "It's one hundred percent beaver fur-felt. This one's called Silver Mist. I thought it would go well with your tux, and you can't wear that hat you've had on since we got to town."

Caleb pulled the taupe hat from his head and studied it. "Why not?"

"Because you work in that hat." Nathan took it from him and tossed it onto the couch behind him. "You're getting married today, and you need a hat to get married in." He extracted the silver hat from the box. "And this is it."

Caleb took the hat from his brother, a swell of emotion rising until it frothed against the back of his tongue. The hat was beautiful, a delicate silver that would compliment his tie and the tips of his shoes—shoes and a tie Holly had chosen for him. She'd chosen silver, navy blue, and yellow for the wedding, and he'd nodded and agreed with whatever she wanted.

"I got a size eight. Seems like that's what you were

wearing a few years ago. I know your head swells from time to time, but…." Nathan trailed off as Caleb looked at him. An understanding passed between them, and Caleb felt closer to his brother than he had in a decade.

"This had to cost eight hundred dollars."

Nathan smiled, a gentle gesture that reached all the way into his eyes and radiated through his soul. "Try it on."

Caleb took an extra moment to run his fingers along the darker gray hatband, which connected with a non-frilly bow. He could definitely wear this to get married. He turned away from Nathan and faced the mirror above the mantle. Somewhat reverently, he placed the hat on his head and adjusted it.

"It's great," he said, his voice a touch on the thick side. Before he could give too much away, he spun back to Nathan and hugged him, clapping him loudly on the back. "Thank you, Nathan."

"I'm glad she makes you happy," Nathan said.

"She does."

Nathan cleared his throat and said, "Then it's time to get down to the church."

"Let me grab my tux, and we'll go."

An hour later, Caleb was dressed, his slacks as seamlessly pressed as his brother's. He tugged at the collar of his shirt, sure whoever had invented tuxedos had done so as a torture device for soon-to-be husbands. Seriously, how did people breathe with buttons so close to their throats?

"Stop pulling at it." Nathan swatted his hands away and added, "It's almost time."

"I've been ready since we got here," Caleb mumbled. Holly's truck had been in the parking lot, but he hadn't been allowed to see her. Nathan had driven him down, as he was leaving with Holly in her truck for a week-long honeymoon in the mountains of Southern Canada.

Someone knocked on the door, and Caleb swung toward it at the same time Nathan opened it. "We're ready for you," someone said, and Caleb tugged on the bottom of his jacket one last time before heading into the chapel.

People filled the rows from front to back; the cowboys from the ranch took up two rows in the front by themselves, with Jace and Belle sitting on one end. His parents surprisingly sat next to Holly's in the front row, and her grandmother had come from Butte. Nathan and Mel sat on the end of the front row, with Eddie on the bench between them. Old classmates and friends of his family's took up the rest of the space, with Dr. Pinnion smiling on them all as Caleb took his place at the altar.

It seemed like a very long time before the organ started playing the wedding march. The doors in the back opened, and Holly appeared, angelic and beautiful in her white dress. A smile sprang to his face and he couldn't erase it no matter how hard he tried.

Every step she took toward him made his heart pound a little harder. A dark, navy blue ribbon wrapped around her waist, tied in the back with a bow with long ends. He wanted to sweep her as close to him as possible, kiss her hello, and tell her how gorgeous she was. How happy she made him. How he hadn't realized how incomplete he was until he'd met her.

She finally arrived at his side and passed off her bouquet, her dark eyes shining with anxiety and excitement and her smile as wide as his. "Hey, pretty lady," he whispered. He reached for her hands and tucked them inside his.

"Nice hat," she whispered back. "Never seen that before."

"It's new."

"You look amazing."

"You steal my breath." He leaned forward, but Dr. Pinnion started speaking, and Caleb straightened. He got to tell Holly all the things he thought about her; he watched as tears welled in her eyes when he said she'd filled a hole in his life he hadn't known was there; he listened as she read her vows to him, as they bound themselves together as husband and wife.

Dr. Pinnion finally said, "You may kiss your bride," and Caleb did what he wanted to do every day of his life.

He kissed his wife.

———

Read on for a sneak peek at **SECOND CHANCE FAMILY**, the next book in the Horseshoe Home Ranch Romance series.

Ty Barker sang along to the radio as he wound down the canyon, Horseshoe Home Ranch in his rearview mirror. He belted out the lyrics, the tune catchy and the singer's voice in the exact range of Ty's capabilities.

The song ended, and Ty slung his arm out the open window, the whole afternoon ahead of him. "That's a good song, right there, Owen," he said, as if the country music star who used to live in Gold Valley rode shotgun next to him. Of course he didn't, but Ty felt a connection to Owen Carr anyway, mostly because he'd been covering the staff horseback riding lessons at Silver Creek since the cowboy left a couple of summers ago.

Everyone Ty knew had found some way to move on, leave him behind. Caleb had gotten married. Jace and Tom too. There were several cowboys at Horseshoe Home that weren't attached, but they all seemed much younger than

Ty, and he definitely felt isolated from the crowd where he'd once fit.

Another song came on, and Ty exchanged his troubled thoughts for the lyrics he had memorized. The sun shone overhead, and everything in Gold Valley seemed carpeted in shades of green, from the sagebrush surrounding the water-falls, to the lawn framing the church, to the trees towering at the park.

A sense of contentment filled Ty at the familiar sight of the only home he'd ever known. He hadn't left and traveled like some did. He hadn't joined the rodeo. He'd never left Gold Valley; couldn't even understand why someone would want to.

Both of his sisters—one older and one younger—had felt the pull to other parts of the country, leaving Ty here to take care of his parents and the house they'd all grown up in. Ty didn't mind. He liked getting away from the ranch, enjoyed an easy afternoon of mowing the lawn and shaping the shrubbery along his parents' front walk. If he could get the morning chores—which no one wanted on Saturdays except for him—he'd stay in town for the weekend dances that happened all summer long.

Tonight, in fact, and a smile stole across his face. He drove through downtown, his gaze wandering to the park where the dance would be later that evening, the weight of needing more committee members pulling on his mind.

A horn sounded, and Ty refocused his attention forward just in time to see the red light. He slammed on his brakes moments before a blue truck sailed in front of him. His head snapped forward and then back, and his heart catapulted to the base of his throat. "Can't dance if you're dead," he muttered to himself, checking both directions before he inched forward again, even though his light had turned green.

He kept his mind on driving for the rest of the way to Silver Creek, where he arrived with a half hour to spare before the riding lessons began. After walking around the barn from the parking lot, he entered it and moved down the row of horses, greeting them all as if they were old friends.

Ty paused outside Pompeii's stall—which was empty. The patients at Silver Creek didn't ride on Saturdays, so the horse shouldn't have been gone. Ty glanced around, his pulse skipping ahead of itself once more.

"Where is he?" he asked a smaller horse named Kimchi. "He's all right, isn't he?" Ty considered horses as much his friends as humans, and his concern for the tall quarter horse spiked.

He vaulted the fence and landed in Pompeii's stall, moving quickly toward the back opening that led to an outdoor arena. Though his boots made clomping noises against the cement, he could distinctly hear the uneven rhythm of horse's hooves as he approached the arena.

Sure enough, a woman rode Pompeii in the arena, her hair fanning out like a fantastic white-blonde curtain behind her. He couldn't see her face, but he could see she didn't quite know how to get Pompeii to do what she wanted. The horse's gait was stilted, and she yanked on the reins when she wanted him to go right, but he didn't.

Ty climbed the rungs on the fence and sat on the top one. "You're squeezin' 'im too tight," he called.

The woman swung toward him, surprise etched across her face. She yelped as Pompeii also turned his attention to Ty—and then headed right for him.

Shock traveled through Ty as the horse rose into a gallop, and he scrambled over the fence just as Pompeii arrived, skidding to a stop and throwing the woman from his back.

Her scream embedded itself into Ty's ears, his mind, his very soul, before she landed right on top of him.

They both collapsed to the ground in a flurry of limbs and grunts. Ty ended up on the bottom, the woman's elbow digging painfully into his ribs, and her knee where no one's knee should ever be.

Ty tried to hold still as pain radiated through his body from sole to skull, but the woman scrambled around, her limbs made of sharp points and sudden movements. He groaned as her elbow made contact with his stomach.

"What was that?" she sputtered, trying desperately to find somewhere to lean her weight that wasn't part of Ty. He'd appreciate that too, to tell the truth. In the end, she pressed both palms against his chest and pushed herself up.

The air rushed from Ty's lungs, and he emitted a strangled sound as she gained her feet and started brushing off her decidedly city clothes. How she could move and breathe in jeans so tight and a blouse so silky almost seemed beyond Ty's reasoning.

He took a few extra seconds to find a decent lungful of air, to realize that the aches in his muscles were just that—aches. Not breaks.

"You were squeezin' 'im too tight," Ty drawled again as he got himself into a seated position. The woman's bright blue eyes seemed so familiar, but he hadn't seen hair so silvery-white on someone her age ever. "I was just trying to help."

"Yeah, help me get thrown."

Pompeii pawed the ground and Ty said, "I wouldn't go back in there quite yet," as the woman started to duck to go under the rungs. He got to his feet and dusted himself down. "He's not interested in riding right now."

"Thanks to you."

Ire rose in Ty. "Who are you? Why are you out here ridin' one of the horses by yourself?"

The woman shook out her hair and squared her shoulders. "I'm new here. I was waiting for the riding instructor, and thought I'd give it a try."

Ty's eyebrows shot up. "You thought you'd give riding a horse *a try?*"

"I rode when I was younger." She rolled her right shoulder—Ty wondered if it ached the way his did—and trained those aquamarine eyes of hers right on his. Ty forgot his own name for a moment. Because he'd suddenly remembered hers.

"River Lee?"

She flinched, and dark shutters drew themselves over those crystal clear eyes. "I go by River now."

Every organ in Ty's body danced the tango. River Lee Whitely had returned to Gold Valley. His heart remembered the last time he'd seen her, and it clenched painfully at the same time hope soared through him.

"River Lee Whitely." He chuckled and shook his head, his usual playfulness rising within him. "You didn't *ride* when you were younger."

"I've been on a horse before, Ty."

So she remembered him too. He wondered if her memories were as strong as his, as saturated with the color and sound of the fair, the taste of that caramel apple they'd shared—and the kiss that followed it.

Ty swallowed hard, his fantasies suddenly overwhelming his memories. "But you didn't ride," he said. "If I remember right, you sat right behind me in the saddle, no work necessary." He slid her a playful smile, wondering—and hoping—it would work as well now as it had fifteen years ago.

Judging by the insta-scowl on her face, his smile had lost some of its charm. A ripple of unease tripped through Ty. "Well," he said. "I'm your riding instructor today, but the lesson doesn't start for another twenty minutes."

---

River blinked at Ty, sure she'd heard him wrong. *He* was her riding instructor? Half of her wanted to march over to the office and demand someone else. She knew it would be pointless. The director of Silver Creek, Dr. Richards, didn't work weekends. The office wasn't even open as only a skeleton staff stayed on-site through the weekends. And she had to be trained with horses to keep the job.

Another set of blue eyes danced through her mind. Her daughter, Lexi's. And another pair: Hannah's. River needed this job, for herself and her two daughters.

She blinked and breathed, and when she looked at Ty again, his stunning, sunny hazel eyes stared back at her, no blue in sight. She could take riding lessons from him. It wasn't like they'd be dating or anything.

"I'll get Pompeii back in his stall." Ty went over the fence, not through it like River was going to, and held the horse's reins in his hand before River had even moved. The horse didn't snort or paw at him, and he spoke to it like it was his grandmother, soothing and low and with a slight coo in his voice.

River shouldn't have been surprised. Ty Barker had always had a way with horses, with dogs—and with girls. River remembered their fun-filled summer together, those hot nights they walked around the town and up to the waterfalls, the single kiss she'd shared with him.

"You comin'?"

She shook herself out of the memory and found him already at the door leading inside. She strode after him despite the hitch of pain in her right ankle and the slight discomfort in her shoulders, wishing she looked more like a resident of Gold Valley instead of where she'd come from: Las Vegas.

At least it was summer in Montana, and she didn't need to buy a whole new wardrobe for a few more months. "Why do we have to take him back?" she asked.

"Well, for starters, you didn't put his saddle on right. So that needs to be redone. And secondly, you're not the only person in the lesson. It's a group lesson, and I was told there were four of you starting today."

"Four of us?" River had only been back in town for a week, and she'd only signed her employment paperwork on Wednesday. She'd start with a group of girls on Monday, and Dr. Richards wanted her to learn to ride a horse over the next twelve weeks—just like the girls did when they came to Silver Creek.

"This place turns over counselors like they're pancakes." Ty led the horse back into his stall while River took the path between two stalls and out to the front of the barn.

"They do?" River hated that everything she'd said had been a question.

"It's a tough job," he said.

Fear boiled inside her, along with a healthy helping of indignation. "Have you done it?"

He laughed, the sound as full and glorious as it had been when River was a teenager. She shivered and a spring of desire to hear his chuckle again bubbled up inside her. She couldn't believe a noise she hadn't heard in a long, long time could elicit such a strong reaction from her. Like the lyrics of a song, his laugh had never left her mind, even if she couldn't recall it at will.

"I work at Horseshoe Home," he said. "I only do this on

the weekends." He scanned her, a hint of something mischievous in his eye. She shifted her feet, noticing how his muscles filled out his shoulders, his arms, his chest. He'd been broad as a sixteen-year-old, but skinny. Now he had the form of a man who worked a ranch and tamed wild horses in his spare time. And she had a new hair color, two daughters under the age of five, and her old bedroom in her parents' house.

"So, what brings you back to town?" he asked as he removed the offensive saddle and redid the work.

River opened her mouth to answer, glad when two other men showed up before she could speak. They both wore cowboy hats and boots, and once again, River felt completely misdressed.

"You must be Ty," one of them said. He shook hands with Ty over the railing and then glanced at River. "I'm Rueben."

Introductions were made, and conversations started, and River did her best to paint her smile in place and speak only when spoken to. Her strategy worked, and before she knew it, Ty had paired her with a much smaller, red-haired horse named, believe it or not, Ole Red.

River's whole body ached by the time she dismounted—clumsily, too. She'd tripped on the stirrup and practically fallen on top of Ty for a second time that day. Her ankle throbbed now, but she'd made it to her car without limping. She would not give Ty the opportunity to tease her, or worse, offer his help.

She didn't need anyone's help, thank you very much. John, her ex-husband, had agreed to have the child support for Lexi and Hannah automatically withdrawn from his hefty paychecks from the law firm in Vegas where he still worked. Still with the same secretary too.

Bitterness coated River's tongue, but it didn't last long. Her marriage had ended eighteen months ago, and the divorce itself was a year old. She'd stayed in Las Vegas out of a legal obligation not to leave the state until everything regarding the girls was settled.

And that had happened a month ago. River had

promptly packed everything they owned and returned to Gold Valley. Her mom had been begging her to come home since the day she'd left for college. A single mother herself, River's mother had been by River's side since the beginning of the split. River wasn't ashamed to admit that she'd been relying on her mom for more than just a place to stay for a while now.

When she pushed into the house with a couple of bags of groceries, she found her two tow-headed girls sitting at the table, a plastic cup of discolored water sitting between them as they painted with watercolors. "Hey, sweeties," she said, removing the tired notes from her voice. She bent over and gave each daughter a quick kiss on the cheek before setting the groceries on the counter. "Where's Grandma?"

Her mother had retired last year, which made the horse-back riding lessons do-able. Or so River had thought.

"She's in the backyard," Lexi said. "Someone came to visit."

River cocked an eyebrow at the sliding glass door that led to the backyard that was her mother's pride and joy. She kept large beds of flowers with lilies, poppies, and roses in a variety of colors. In the far left corner, she'd planted several lilac bushes and two bleeding heart trees that River had grown up loving. She often hid behind the lilacs in the summer when she wanted to be alone, breathing in their fragrance and trying to figure out what to do with her life.

With the strong urge to lose herself in that scent again, River stepped to the door and slid it open. "Stay here, girls. I'll be right back to make dinner." She'd just come in from the heated afternoon, but the sweat on her brow had barely cooled in the weak air conditioning.

"Mom?" She glanced around but didn't see her mother. The grass stretched before her like an emerald carpet, and Pippa, her mother's white terrier yipped and came trotting around the shed that sat under the towering bur oak tree. Her little legs pumped as she crossed the lawn.

"Hey, Pip." River scooped up the little, fifteen-pound dog and added, "Where's Mommy, huh?"

As the seconds stretched, River's anxiety expanded. Surely her mother wouldn't just wander off and leave her two granddaughters in the house alone. Just as she was about to return to the house and call her mother—and then the Sheriff—the door to the shed flew open and banged against the building.

Her mother exited, a wide smile on her face. Her trilling laugh echoed through the quiet neighborhood, easing River's worry—until she saw the tall, broad cowboy who ducked to exit the shed behind her mother.

Then she could only see red. She stomped toward the shed, where Ty stood with a shovel slung over his shoulder, that knee-weakening smile adorning his beautiful mouth.

"What are you doing here?" she demanded.

He switched his happy gaze to hers, and she remembered how jovial he'd always been. Some might even call him a prankster, though he never did anything harmful. At least that he'd been caught for.

"Hey, River Lee," he said easily, like he hadn't given her the best kiss of her life and then broken up with her.

"It's just River," she ground between her teeth. "And you didn't answer my question."

"I wanted to ask you something, but you weren't here." He glanced at River's mom. "And your mom asked me to do some yard work for her."

River switched her glare to her mother, the traitor. "You don't need any yard work done."

Her mother lifted her chin, her blue eyes as dangerous as Ty's dark ones. Glittering just as much too. "Yes, I do. I haven't been able to get that faucet to stop leaking. Ty said he could do it."

River stared past the two of them to the spigot in the back of the yard, surrounded by white, decorative rocks. Her gaze landed back on Ty, who had taken the smile from knee-weakening to bone-melting. "With a shovel?" she asked, a definite bite of acid in her question.

He tipped his hat, said, "You never know when you'll need a shovel," and strode toward the leaking faucet.

"Mom," River hissed as Pippa began squirming in her arms. She set the little dog down and she tore after Ty. "How long has he been here?"

She didn't take her eyes from Ty's back. "I don't know. Fifteen minutes? The girls are inside."

"I saw them." River spun and retraced her steps back to the house. Did her mother honestly think River wanted to start dating again?

*Maybe if the man asking is Ty Barker.*

She almost tripped over her own feet at the way her brain betrayed her. She gave herself a shake and practically ripped the sliding glass door off its track. Once inside the house, her chest heaved as if she'd just run a marathon. She wasn't even sure why. The faucet *had* been leaking since the irrigation water had come back on, but it wasn't like her mother had even tried to fix it herself. She just hadn't gotten around to it, what with River and her daughters moving in with such little notice.

She yanked the groceries out of the bags and picked up a chef's knife to chop the onions she needed for the sloppy Joes. Hannah giggled, and River's anger deflated.

"Pippa," the little girl said, sliding off her chair and straining to open the sliding glass door. River let her have the chance to let the dog in, smiling with pride when Hannah got the door open and beamed in River's direction.

"Good job, baby," River said, her dialect already returning to the small-town, western way of talking she'd left behind long ago.

"I cook too?" Hannah toddled into the kitchen, and River pulled over the chair she'd been sitting on. After lifting Hannah onto it and setting a heavy pan on the stove, she gave her a wooden spoon.

"You stir." She mimicked moving the spoon around the pan and turned back to the counter to collect the chopped onions. They sizzled as they hit the pan, and Hannah started stirring the way River had shown her.

River added salt and pepper, as well as a hunk of butter, and stepped around Hannah to open the fridge. She'd collected the ground beef, the mustard, and the chili sauce before she heard voices approaching.

A low, masculine one that sent shivers down her spine and her mother's higher timbre that grated against River's nerves. Truth be told, she was just as annoyed at herself for finding every single thing about Ty so darn attractive.

She eyed him as he entered the house and took in the scene before him: Lexi painting at the table, the same eyes and nose as River. And Hannah standing at the stove, her hair the exact same color as River's, even if River's came from multiple steps only a talented stylist could achieve.

"Beef," River said quietly as she turned her back on Ty and started crumbling the beef into the pan so Hannah could stir it around. "Mix it all up, 'kay?" She steadfastly refused to look at Ty as she got out a bottle of apple cider vinegar and a sack of brown sugar.

He had come by to ask her something, but she didn't want to talk to him. Over the past couple of years, River had gotten very good at ignoring uncomfortable things and making light of awkward situations.

She'd also learned how to talk about how she felt, and she'd already looked for a therapist here in Gold Valley that could continue to help her heal emotionally.

"Can I talk to you for a sec?" Ty seemed to appear magically at his side, as if he'd teleported there.

River's fingers stumbled on the twist tie keeping the brown sugar fresh. Instead of trying to rectify her mistake, she simply abandoned the task. "Mom? Can you stand here by Hannah?" The beef needed to brown, and that was at least five or six minutes away.

"Sure thing." Her mom edged into the kitchen as Ty slid

his way out. He walked into the living room, but didn't stop there. He opened the front door stepped onto the porch.

River warred with herself. She could rush to the door and lock it, sending a clear and loud message to Ty—the way he had all those summers ago.

*Don't burn bridges*, echoed in her mind. One of her mother's life lessons. One that had actually stuck in River's mind. One she'd relied on throughout college, her counseling internship, even her failed marriage.

She coached herself that just because Ty was good-looking didn't mean she had to let him into her life. That just because she'd kissed him before didn't mean she had to do it again. That just because he wanted to talk didn't mean she had to listen.

She lifted her shoulders and joined him on the front porch. "What's up?"

Ty leaned against the porch railing, seemingly at ease right here where he hadn't been for a while. "So just hear me out."

It took every ounce of River's willpower not to lean her elbows next to his, share the same air as him, take a deep drag of his intoxicating scent. "All right."

"All right," he drawled, mimicking her. "You sound like you haven't left at all." He chuckled but sobered quickly. "So I help out with the summer activities. Specifically, I'm in charge of the children's carnival during the Fourth of July week, the end-of-summer carnival, and the weekend dances."

River tried to bite down on the information and chew

on it for a moment before speaking, but trying to imagine Ty planning events was so far from who she thought he was. "You're doing what?" she asked with no small measure of incredulity.

His shoulders stiffened and he ducked his chin to put the brim of his cowboy hat between them. "I volunteer on a community service committee," he said. "And we need more help. I thought maybe you'd like to join up. Help out with the kid's activities or the carnival or the dances."

She laughed, the sound anything but carefree and happy. "I don't think so." She'd be working with a group of eight teen girls come Monday, and then returning home to care for her own two daughters. She didn't think she'd even have enough mental stamina to do that, let alone think about what other people's children would like to see and do at an Independence Day activity.

And helping with the carnival? Definitely out. Just thinking about such things made the taste of caramel coat her tongue and her lips tingle from the once-gentle pressure of Ty's mouth against hers.

No, she could absolutely not help him organize anything having to do with the carnival. No, sirree.

She'd known about the dances in Gold Valley's central square. She'd attended as a teenager, spun with several boys before she left for college, even snuck off to kiss one of them after the last dance of the summer.

River glanced at Ty, wondering if those memories, that summer, his words, ever haunted him.

"You don't have to do all of that," Ty said. "Just one thing would suffice. Or I know Doris Downing needs help with the judging for the county fair. Baked goods and sewing."

The way he wouldn't look at her drove frustration through her bloodstream. At the same time, she didn't want his powerful gaze on her, sure she'd wilt beneath the magnificence of his murky, pond water-colored eyes.

He waited with all the patience of a monk, and River couldn't stand to be in the same space as him for much longer. "Thanks, but no thanks." She twisted, entered the house, and closed the door behind her.

Exhaling, she leaned into the door and pressed her eyes closed. *Dear Lord*, she prayed. *How am I going to survive living in Gold Valley with Ty Barker?*

God didn't have an answer for her, and River felt as though she'd been stung by an army of red ants. She thought she'd be able to find a new start in Gold Valley. Thought she'd be able to find peace away from the hustle and bustle of the big cities where she used to live. Thought she'd be able to build a life for her girls and raise them with good values.

She had not even considered that Ty would still be in town, though she should have known better. A country boy at heart, she couldn't imagine Ty anywhere with more people than cattle. A city like Las Vegas would swallow him whole. It had River, and she loved a thriving city, with more than one grocery store and highways and byways that criss-crossed the metropolis.

"Mama," Hannah said, and River opened her eyes, choosing to put one foot in front of the other, just like she had when she'd left Las Vegas. Along with that, she believed if she kept her faith in the Lord, He'd guide her where she needed to go.

She scraped her hair off her forehead and gave Hannah a tired smile. "Look at what you've done, baby doll." She stroked the little girl's hair and said, "Now we add everything and then you'll keep stirring."

———

Ty's disappointment over River's laughter and subsequent rejection wafted behind him like a foul scent. His mother noticed when he arrived at their house, and she questioned him relentlessly until he muttered something about the lawn and escaped to the backyard.

Honestly, he wasn't sure why he'd thought asking River to get involved with community service was a good idea. He just knew he'd felt like he should, so he'd jumped in his truck and gone to her mother's house. Seeing the two blonde girls hanging onto their grandmother's legs had taken the wind right out of his sails. And yet, he'd still asked River if she'd wanted to help, as if she didn't already have her hands full.

The roar of the lawnmower kept Ty's mutterings mute to the rest of the world. As he berated himself for such grand notions, he clipped his parents' yard to pure perfection. He showered, and denied his mother the opportunity to feed him dinner—a rare occurrence indeed. If she hadn't known something was off then, she certainly would've when he bypassed the homemade waffles and plate of bacon.

"What's wrong?" She put her hands on her hips and cocked her head at him, her dark eyes blazing with determination.

"Nothin', Ma. Don't want to talk about it." He picked up a waffle and smeared peanut butter on it like it was a piece of bread. "I will eat here."

"Everything okay at the ranch?"

"Nothing ever changes at the ranch." He took a big bite of his waffle sandwich, thinking he should just tell him mom about River Lee. She'd find out anyway, and if he just blurted it out, he wouldn't have to endure the questioning.

"The riding lessons, then?" She spoke with a quietness in her tone but with eyes so sharp they cut right through Ty's defenses.

He shook his head, swallowed, and said, "Did you know River Lee Whitely is back in town? And that she has two daughters?"

Everything about his mom softened. She glanced over Ty's shoulder as his dad entered the kitchen. "I had heard she was back, yes."

"Who's back?" His dad slid a waffle onto a plate and slathered it with butter.

"River Lee Whitely," his mom said before Ty could somehow communicate with her nonverbally.

"River Lee?" His dad abandoned his waffle prep and pinned Ty with a look. "You're still hung up on her?"

Ty grabbed a handful of bacon and put it on a plate. "I was never 'hung up' on her, Dad."

"You were sneakin' out all the time to see her."

"Once," Ty said. "I snuck out once. And it wasn't like I was twelve years old."

"Doesn't matter how old you were." He spooned sugared strawberries onto his waffle. "Bein' older is worse. No control over your hormones."

Ty scoffed and took his food to the table. His mom watched the exchange with too much interest, and Ty had the urge to get out of the house as quickly as possible. He shoved the rest of his waffle in his mouth and chewed with vigor. The waffle scraped his throat as he practically swallowed it whole.

"I have to go."

"Have fun," his mom said, while his dad added, "Be good."

Ty waved to indicate that he'd heard them, but every step he took was fueled by frustration. So he'd snuck out once to meet River Lee at the drive-in. He didn't have a car, but she did. Nothing had happened. In fact, he'd barely slipped his fingers between hers before his dad had pounded on the window and demanded Ty get out of the sedan.

Even after that embarrassing incident, River Lee had still been interested in him. If only she hadn't said she couldn't wait to leave Gold Valley. Couldn't wait to start college. Couldn't wait to "get on with her life."

She'd told him all of that after he'd taken her on the

Ferris wheel, after he'd bought a caramel apple to share, after they'd danced around the square, after they'd snuck off to a secret spot behind the rodeo stands and kissed. They'd found a patch of grass illuminated by the moonlight and lay in each other's arms, whispering secrets until long past his curfew.

And she'd done exactly what she'd said she wanted to do. She'd left Gold Valley. She'd gone to college. She'd gotten on with her life.

A life that didn't include him.

Even after he'd kissed her, she hadn't made room for him in her life. He'd held her anyway, smiled at her dreams anyway, told her he'd see her later anyway.

And he had seen her. But he hadn't touched her again. Hadn't kissed her more than that one, magical time behind the rodeo stands, her words always a barrier between them. Then…but maybe not now.

A smile graced Ty's face, and he wondered if maybe God had led River Lee home right when she was supposed to be here.

He arrived at the park and helped set up the refreshment tables, the dance floor, and the sound equipment for the band. It was a big job for only a handful of people, and he was certain everything would be easier with only one more pair of hands.

River Lee's hands.

*Forget about it, Ty,* he told himself just before a brunette launched herself at him with a squeal and the strength of a python in her legs as she wrapped them around his body.

"There you are," she said with more flirt in her voice than anything else. "I've missed you."

Ty held onto Whitney, because he had little other choice. Number one, he didn't want to drop the girl. Number two, technically, one could say they were dating. Ty had asked her to dance two weeks ago, and then taken her for ice cream afterward. And at last week's shindig, he hadn't danced with anyone but her and they'd gone stargazing at the waterfalls after the festivities ended.

But with the reappearance of River Lee in his life, he'd completely, one-hundred percent forgotten about Whitney. He groaned and pretended it was because of her body attached to his. But really, it was the sound of his heart dying just a little bit.

---

**Read SECOND CHANCE FAMILY today!** A handsome cowboy, a single mother, and a second chance for these high school sweethearts...

Scan the QR code on the next page to get it!

**The Redesigned Ranch (Book 1):** Jace Lovell, still nursing a wounded heart after being jilted at the altar, has dedicated himself to becoming the best foreman at Horseshoe Home Ranch. When he decides to hire an interior designer to please the ranch owner's wife, he didn't expect to be faced with a familiar face from his past. **Can Belle's patience and faith help Jace find the path to forgiveness and lead them to discover their own slice of happily-ever-after?**

**Snowed in with the Cowboy (Book 2):** Sterling Maughan, once a renowned snowboarder, is in self-imposed exile at his family cabin after a tragic accident stole his career. Lost and without purpose, solitude is his only companion until an unexpected visitor disrupts his isolation. **Can Norah trust Sterling enough to let him into her life and give their unexpected and forbidden love a chance?**

**The Preacher's Daughter (Book 3):** Landon Edmunds, a cowboy born and bred, has had his rodeo dreams realized and then dashed by a career-ending injury. Back in his hometown working at Horseshoe Home Ranch, he yearns for a new beginning with a ranch of his own. His sights are set on buying a horse ranch to train rodeo horses, but his plans take a detour when his high school best friend, Megan Palmer, steps back into his life. **Will they choose to follow their hearts, or will they let true love slip through their fingers again?**

*Be sure to check out the spinoff series, the Brush Creek Cowboys romances after you read THE PREACHER'S DAUGHTER. Start with BRUSH CREEK COWBOY.*

**The Cowboy and the Nanny(Book 4):** Twelve years ago, Owen Carr traded his roots and his sweetheart in Gold Valley for the bright lights of Nashville, where he found fame as a country music star. But when a tragic accident leaves him single-handedly raising his eight-year-old niece, Marie, he's forced to return home. Overwhelmed and out of his depth, Owen finds a lifeline in a most unexpected place. **As they mend bridges and explore the sparks that still sizzle between them, will they open their hearts to a second chance at love?**

**Right Cowboy, Right Time (Book 5):** Caleb Chamberlain, a fun-loving cowboy at Horseshoe Home Ranch, has spent the last five years wrestling with the ghosts of his past—a devastating breakup, alcoholism, and a near-fatal accident. Now, he's finally found solace in laughter and the rhythmic simplicity of ranch life. But a chance encounter with a familiar face threatens to upheave his newfound peace. **Can they navigate the shadows of the past to find their happily-ever-after?**

**Second Chance Family (Book 6):** Ty Barker has been living a carefree existence for the last thirty years. As friends around him found love and started families, Ty filled his time by giving horseback riding lessons and serving on a community service committee. But beneath the jovial surface, he's starting to feel the sting of loneliness. **He knows he wants River Lee in his life—but the question is, can he navigate the delicate steps needed to make her stay with him?**

**The Christmas Cowboy Competition (Book 7):** Archer Bailey has already had to yield one job to Emersyn "Emery" Enders. So when the opportunity of a cowhand job at Horseshoe Home Ranch presents itself, he keeps it to himself. Emery, whose temporary job is ending but whose responsibilities towards her physically disabled sister aren't, is left in the dark.

As the festive season unfolds, **will Emery and Archer navigate the complexities of the ranch, their close living arrangements, and their personal challenges to discover the love building between them? Or will their rivalry rob them of the greatest Christmas gift of all—true love?**

**Love at First Cowboy (Book 8):** Elliott Hawthorne, a career cowboy, has just witnessed his best friend and cabinmate forsake bachelorhood for matrimony. He'd be joyous if he weren't so green with envy. When a call about a family accident demands his presence, Elliott finds himself rushing from the ranch to his parents' house to see what's going on with his daddy, where he encounters the most stunning woman he's ever laid eyes on. **But as they encounter the complex dynamics of family responsibilities and personal desires, can their love-at-first-sight grow strong enough withstand the test of time?**

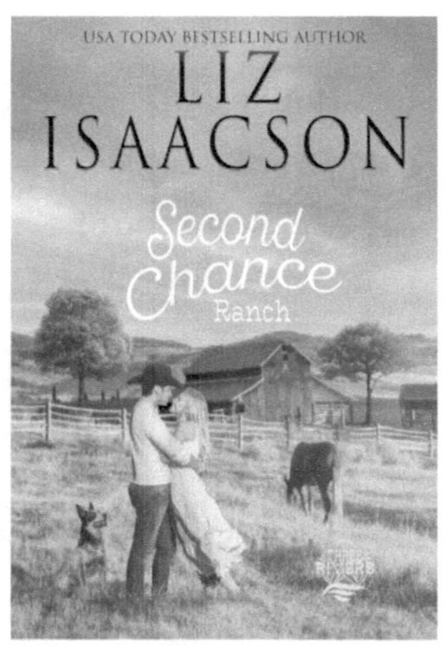

**Second Chance Ranch: A Three Rivers Ranch Romance™ (Book 1):** After his deployment, injured and discharged Major Squire Ackerman returns to Three Rivers Ranch, wanting to forgive Kelly for ignoring him a decade ago. He'd like to provide the stable life she needs, but with old wounds opening and a ranch on the brink of financial collapse, it will take patience and faith to make their second chance possible.

**Third Time's the Charm: A Three Rivers Ranch Romance™ (Book 2):** First Lieutenant Peter Marshall has a truckload of debt and no way to provide for a family, but Chelsea helps him see past all the obstacles, all the scars. With so many unknowns, can Pete and Chelsea develop the love, acceptance, and faith needed to find their happily ever after?

**Fourth and Long: A Three Rivers Ranch Romance™ (Book 3):** Commander Brett Murphy goes to Three Rivers Ranch to find some rest and relaxation with his Army buddies. Having his ex-wife show up with a seven-year-old she claims is his son is anything but the R&R he craves. Kate needs to make amends, and Brett needs to find forgiveness, but are they too late to find their happily ever after?

**Fifth Generation Cowboy: A Three Rivers Ranch Romance™ (Book 4):** Tom Lovell has watched his friends find their true happiness on Three Rivers Ranch, but everywhere he looks, he only sees friends. Rose Reyes has been bringing her daughter out to the ranch for equine therapy for months, but it doesn't seem to be working. Her challenges with Mari are just as frustrating as ever. Could Tom be exactly what Rose needs? Can he remove his friendship blinders and find love with someone who's been right in front of him all this time?

**Sixth Street Love Affair: A Three Rivers Ranch Romance™ (Book 5):** After losing his wife a few years back, Garth Ahlstrom thinks he's ready for a second chance at love. But Juliette Thompson has a secret that could destroy their budding relationship. Can they find the strength, patience, and faith to make things work?

**The Seventh Sergeant: A Three Rivers Ranch Romance™ (Book 6):** Life has finally started to settle down for Sergeant Reese Sanders after his devastating injury overseas. Discharged from the Army and now with a good job at Courage Reins, he's finally found happiness—until a horrific fall puts him right back where he was years ago: Injured and depressed. Carly Watters, Reese's new veteran care coordinator, dislikes small towns almost as much as she loathes cowboys. But she finds herself faced with both when she gets assigned to Reese's case. Do they have the humility and faith to make their relationship more than professional?

**Eight Second Ride: A Three Rivers Ranch Romance™ (Book 7):** Ethan Greene loves his work at Three Rivers Ranch, but he can't seem to find the right woman to settle down with. When sassy yet vulnerable Brynn Bowman shows up at the ranch to recruit him back to the rodeo circuit, he takes a different approach with the barrel racing champion. His patience and newfound faith pay off when a friendship--and more--starts with Brynn. But she wants out of the rodeo circuit right when Ethan wants to rejoin. Can they find the path God wants them to take and still stay together?

**The Ninth Inning: A Three Rivers Ranch Romance™ (Book 8):** The Christmas season has never felt like such a burden to boutique owner Andrea Larsen. But with Mama gone and the holidays upon her, Andy finds herself wishing she hadn't been so quick to judge her former boyfriend, cowboy Lawrence Collins. Well, Lawrence hasn't forgotten about Andy either, and he devises a plan to get her out to the ranch so they can reconnect. Do they have the faith and humility to patch things up and start a new relationship?

**Ten Days in Town: A Three Rivers Ranch Romance™ (Book 9):** Sandy Keller is tired of the dating scene in Three Rivers. Though she owns the pancake house, she's looking for a fresh start, which means an escape from the town where she grew up. When her older brother's best friend, Tad Jorgensen, comes to town for the holidays, it is a balm to his weary soul. A helicopter tour guide who experienced a near-death experience, he's looking to start over too--but in Three Rivers. Can Sandy and Tad navigate their troubles to find the path God wants them to take--and discover true love--in only ten days?

**Eleven Year Reunion: A Three Rivers Ranch Romance™ (Book 10):** Pastry chef extraordinaire, Grace Lewis has moved to Three Rivers to help Heidi Ackerman open a bakery in Three Rivers. Grace relishes the idea of starting over in a town where no one knows about her failed cupcakery. She doesn't expect to run into her old high school boyfriend, Jonathan Carver. A carpenter working at Three Rivers Ranch, Jon's in town against his will. But with Grace now on the scene, Jon's thinking life in Three Rivers is suddenly looking up. But with her focus on baking and his disdain for small towns, can they make their eleven year reunion stick?

**The Twelfth Town: A Three Rivers Ranch Romance™ (Book 11):** Newscaster Taryn Tucker has had enough of life on-screen. She's bounced from town to town before arriving in Three Rivers, completely alone and completely anonymous-- just the way she now likes it. She takes a job cleaning at Three Rivers Ranch, hoping for a chance to figure out who she is and where God wants her. When she meets happy-go-lucky cowhand Kenny Stockton, she doesn't expect sparks to fly. Kenny's always been "the best friend" for his female friends, but the pull between him and Taryn can't be denied. Will they have the courage and faith necessary to make their opposite worlds mesh?

**Lucky Number Thirteen: A Three Rivers Ranch Romance™ (Book 12):** Tanner Wolf, a rodeo champion ten times over, is excited to be riding in Three Rivers for the first time since he left his philandering ways and found religion. Seeing his old friends Ethan and Brynn is therapuetic--until a terrible accident lands him in the hospital. With his rodeo career over, Tanner thinks maybe he'll stay in town--and it's not just because his nurse, Summer Hamblin, is the prettiest woman he's ever met. But Summer's the queen of first dates, and as she looks for a way to make a relationship with the transient rodeo star work Summer's not sure she has the fortitude to go on a second date. Can they find love among the tragedy?

**The Curse of February Fourteenth: A Three Rivers Ranch Romance™ (Book 13):** Cal Hodgkins, cowboy veterinarian at Bowman's Breeds, isn't planning to meet anyone at the masked dance in small-town Three Rivers. He just wants to get his bachelor friends off his back and sit on the sidelines to drink his punch. But when he sees a woman dressed in gorgeous butterfly wings and cowgirl boots with blue stitching, he's smitten. Too bad she runs away from the dance before he can get her name, leaving only her boot behind...

**Fifteen Minutes of Fame: A Three Rivers Ranch Romance™ (Book 14):** Navy Richards is thirty-five years of tired—tired of dating the same men, working a demanding job, and getting her heart broken over and over again. Her aunt has always spoken highly of the matchmaker in Three Rivers, Texas, so she takes a six-month sabbatical from her high-stress job as a pediatric nurse, hops on a bus, and meets with the matchmaker. Then she meets Gavin Redd. He's handsome, he's hardworking, and he's a cowboy. But is he an Aquarius too? Navy's not making a move until she knows for sure...

**Sixteen Steps to Fall in Love: A Three Rivers Ranch Romance™ (Book 15):** A chance encounter at a dog park sheds new light on the tall, talented Boone that Nicole can't ignore. As they get to know each other better and start to dig into each other's past, Nicole is the one who wants to run. This time from her growing admiration and attachment to Boone. From her aging parents. From herself.

But Boone feels the attraction between them too, and he decides he's tired of running and ready to make Three Rivers his permanent home. **Can Boone and Nicole use their faith to overcome their differences and find a happily-ever-after together?**

**The First Lady of Three Rivers Ranch: A Three Rivers Ranch Romance™ (Book 17):** Heidi Duffin has been dreaming about opening her own bakery since she was thirteen years old. She scrimped and saved for years to afford baking and pastry school in San Francisco. And now she only has one year left before she's a certified pastry chef.

Frank Ackerman's father has recently retired, and he's taken over the largest cattle ranch in the Texas Panhandle. A horseman through and through, he's also nearing thirty-one and looking for someone to bring love and joy to a homestead that's been dominated by men for a decade. But when he convinces Heidi to come clean the cowboy cabins, she changes all that. But the siren's call of a bakery is still loud in Heidi's ears, even if she's also seeing a future with Frank. Can she rely on her faith in ways she's never had to before or will their relationship end when summer does?

**Eighteen Bowties and Counting: A Three Rivers Ranch Romance™ (Book 18):** He's her older brother's best friend and completely off-limits. She's got a way with horses...and a heart condition. Can Beau and Charlotte navigate close quarters to find their happily-ever-after?

# ABOUT LIZ

Liz Isaacson writes inspirational romance, usually set in Texas, or Wyoming, or anywhere else horses and cowboys exist. She lives in Utah, where she writes full-time, takes her two dogs to the park everyday, and eats a lot of veggies while writing. Find her on her website at feelgoodfiction-books.com